**DIRTY
DONS**

BOUGHT
By The Don

CARLY DAVIS

Contents

I saved her… hid her from the world. My Jewel was camouflaged from my enemies. For years, I wondered if I did the right thing. Was the family I left her with taking good care of her? When I enter the auction, I get my answer. I never expected to see her big blue eyes. And never expected for her to be the main attraction. Virgin for sale… highest bidder wins. I had no intention of buying her, but her body called to me. I find myself bidding. Again and again. Until I'm the proud owner of an eighteen year old virgin. She thinks I saved her again. She so wrong. I just threw her to the hungry wolf. I'm going to enjoy breaking my Jewel down. Piece by piece. But not before I seek out the family that promised to protect her and get my revenge.

Prologue

Vadim

In my world, you kill or be killed. That's why I'm feared. I kill. Torture. I'm not a good man. Just a Devil in an expensive suit. A monster.

My second-in-command bursts into my office dragging a dark-haired teenager. "Found the girl, boss. What do you want me to do with her?"

"Take her to Regina and have her clean the girl up." I replied.

The girl raised her head, piercing me with her frightened blue eyes. Her lips quivered as tears rolled down her cheeks. She was scared and had a right to be. Just as Alexei was about to take her away, I said. "Wait."

I stood up and walked around the desk, holding up my hand to Alexei. "Leave us for a moment."
Alexei nods and steps out of the room, leaving just the girl and I.

"What is your name, girl?" I demanded.

"Please, Sir. Please, don't hurt me." She whispered.
I put two fingers under her chin, forcing her to look me directly in the eyes. "Tell me your name."

"Jewel, Sir."

I already knew who she was.
Just needed to hear it from her.

"Jewel," I drawled out. "Nobody is going to hurt you. I'm going to get you cleaned up and give you a hot meal. You will stay with me until I find you a proper family. I'm not going to have any problems out of you, no?"

"N-no, Sir," She stuttered, her cheeks flushing pink.

"Good girl," I murmured, "I want you to go with Alexei and get cleaned up. When you're finished, he'll bring you to my room to eat."

I took her gently by the wrist and led her to the door. She was scared. Trembling with fear. Before I opened it, I leaned down and whispered to her. "Trust me, nobody is going to hurt you with me around. I promise."

I open the door and narrowed my eyes at Alexei. "Make sure she gets cleaned up. Bring her straight to my room after."

He furrowed his brows in confusion. "Boss?"

"You heard me," I tell him.

Alexei sighed but did as I asked. I watched them leave the room and ran a hand over my face.

What am I doing?

Jewel had been found down at the club hiding in the office. After digging, I found out she was my best friend's kid sister. Last night, Luciano, her brother had been gunned down. Before he died, he made me promise to take care of his sister. He wanted her to live a normal life. Little did I know, I already had her in my possession. She tried to run. Hence, why Alexei busted in my office.

I made a few calls to find Jewel a good family. With that being done, I headed towards my bedroom and quickly changed out of my suit. Just a pair of sweats and white t-shirt would do.

Knock. Knock.

"Enter," I say, my voice harsh.

One of my maids rolled a cart into the room and bowed her head.

"Thank you, you're dismissed."

About twenty minutes later, Alexei deposits Jewel to me. I had to look twice. This wasn't a girl in the dirty white dress I met over an hour ago. Her pale skin was washed and her matted brunette hair was braided to one side. She looked like an Angel.

"Come, Jewel," I extended my arm for her to take my hand. "I've got dinner ready. Roast with fresh vegetables sautéed in garlic butter."

I expect her to cower, but she doesn't. Jewel takes my hand without hesitation. I tense when she launched herself at me. She hugged me tight and whispered. "Thank you for saving me, Sir."

If only you knew, Angel.

I didn't save her out of the kindness of my heart.

"Sit down and eat. I'll go over the rules."

I led her to the bed by the small of her back and forced her to sit. I pushed the cart closer and glanced at Alexei.

"Rule number one: Always do as I say."

"What's rule number two?" Jewel asked, her mouth full of food.

"There is only one rule. Be a good girl, Jewel. If you obey me, we won't have a problem. Any other questions?"

"No… I mean, yes, Sir."

I raised my brow in question.

Jewel leaned forward and whispered. "What if I'm not a good girl, Sir?"

Fuck me.

"If you're a bad girl, I suppose you would get punished."

Excitement lights up in her eyes when punished rolled off my tongue.

"Be good and eat your dinner. I'll be right back."

I followed Alexei out of the room and sighed. Alexei folded his arms over his chest and narrowed his eyes. "I don't like this. Do you have any idea who that is?"

"Yes," I hissed, "And that's why I have to send her away. She will be protected under a new identity. Nobody will ever know she existed. I promised Luciano to keep her safe."

"Boss…"

"My mind is made up. I have to get rid of her."

Alexei shook his head and nodded behind me.

"Y-you're g-gonna kill me?" I hear Jewel croak out.

I glared at Alexei before turning on my heels. I met her tear-stricken eyes and softened my gaze. For some reason, it hurt to see her cry. Her blue eyes pierced me in my chest. An ache I'd never felt.

"I'm not going to kill you," I assured her.

"You're going to send me away?"

"It's for the best, little one. I'm going to find you a good family to give you a normal life."

"Will I ever see you again, Sir?"

"Vadim," I say, "My name is Vadim Kaslov. And to answer your question, perhaps we'll meet again."

For her sake, I hope we don't see each other again. Because if I see her baby blues again, I'll know I failed her. I owed it to her and Luciano.

Chapter 1

Jules

Two years later

"Jules, come here." I hear my adoptive mother say.

I stepped into the front room and saw my parents sitting with an older man.

"Honey, this is Yuri Volkov. Come and say hello." My father says.

Yuri licked his lips, scanning my body. His hard gaze took me in. From head to toe. I hugged myself to hide, averting my gaze.

"Jules," my mother snapped, "It's rude to look away. Quit being a spoiled brat and say hello to our guest."

"It's okay," Yuri drawled out, "She'll learn obedience and respect."

Learn?
Obedience and respect?

"I'm going out with Sarah tonight. She's taking me out to celebrate my birthday."

"That's right, you're eighteen, yes?" Yuri states.

I nodded.

My father forced a smile while my mother pressed her lips into a thin line. Yuri stood up and walked towards me until he's just an inch from my face. His large hand gripped my wrist and jerked me to his chest. Yuri's free arm wrapped around my waist and leaned into my neck to whisper to me. "Be careful out there tonight. You never know who's watching you."

His words send a chill down my spine. Something tells me he's not warning me. It's a direct threat. A promise that he's going to find me later.

Yuri pulled away and reached inside his pocket. In the palm of his hand is a gold necklace with a red jewel dangling from it. He slides it over my neck and smiled in satisfaction. "Happy birthday, my precious jewel. Until we meet again."

"What do we say to Yuri?" My mother sneered.

"T-thank you, Mr. Volkov."

Yuri pulled away thankfully. His next words made my stomach turn.

"Make sure she keeps her hymen intact. Remember the deal. No virgin… no money."

No virgin… no money?
What was happening?

"O-of course, Mr. Volkov." My father stuttered.

"Good. I'll be in touch very, very soon. Sooner than you think." Yuri says, never taking his eyes off me.

Something about him reminds me of Vadim. A dark and dangerous edge to his voice and gaze. Just as Yuri walked out the front door, he looked over his shoulder smiled darkly.

I turned only to grabbed by the waist and a hand clamped over my mouth. I clawed and tried to scream. It was no use. My father's cold, dark eyes pierced into me. "I'm sorry, but it's for the best."

My mother stepped forward, wielding a syringe. I struggle to break free as tears roll down my face. My heart pounds. My father overpowered me. The last thing I see is my mother jabbing a needle in my neck. Pain. Then… darkness.

"Mmm," I groaned in pain, "Where am I?"

I try to sit up to find I've been restrained. My wrists are tied behind my back and my ankles are zip tied together. I screamed out only to have a rag stuffed in my mouth. I try to spit it out, but the man slaps duct tape over my lips.

The man stroked my cheek and said. "So beautiful. It's a shame I can't touch you. I would've loved to hear you scream when I break through your hymen."

"Quit messing around and drug her. Boss wants this one nice and docile." Another voice hissed.

I whimpered through the rag as I'm injected for the second time. My vision blurred as man number one carries me outside and threw me in the back of the van. When I come to, I'm in a dark room with only a candle as a light. I attempt to sit up and begin to panic when I realized I'm strapped to the bed. My chest heaves in panic when I look down at my body. I've been stripped naked with only the necklace left on me. I widen my eyes when I hear footsteps approaching. A man stepped into the light and smiled as he admired my body.

Yuri licked his lips as he loosened his tie and sat on the edge of the bed. The more I struggled to break free; the more it amused him.

"Such a precious jewel. He murmured, "Just as beautiful as I imagined you to be. You'll make a fine addition as the pawn in my game."

Yuri jammed a needle in my arm, injecting me in the vein. I expect to lose consciousness, but I don't. I feel my heartbeat accelerate as heat and arousal spread throughout me. A small moan escapes my lips as Yuri wrapped his hand around my neck.

"Please, Mr. Volkov." I begged.

"You feel that, yes?"

Yuri loosened his grip and slides his hand down my chest. Between his thumb and index finger, he takes my nipple and gives it a sharp pinch. I cried out only to be slapped.

"Quiet, little girl."

"Fuck you."

Yuri raised his hand again to slap me, but one of his men interrupted him. "Boss, are you ready for me?"

"Yes. Pierce her nipples and clit. And make sure you gag her. This one… she's a screamer."

***

"And now ladies and gentlemen, the main event. May I present Jules, pure and untouched."

My eyelids flutter, my vision hazy from the drugs. All I see is a room full of people. My wrists are chained above my head and my ankles are shackled. I'm dressed in nothing but a red, sheer robe. It's transparent. My nipples and clit throb from being pierced. Compliments of Yuri Volkov.

I scan the room and that's when I see them. Cold, dark eyes searing into my soul. Vadim is seated in the back. Same expensive suit. He's sipping his wine. And next to him is Alexei. Also sipping wine.

"This is Jules, eighteen years old. She would make the perfect toy to satisfy you. Of course, this one isn't trained yet. That's why this one is special. She's Russian and very much a virgin. Starting bid will be at one hundred thousand dollars."

Vadim seems different. Darker and colder. Sexy too. I feel desire burning inside me as Vadim never takes his eyes off me. Vadim lifts his number.

"One hundred. Anyone go higher?"

To my surprise, Vadim lifts his number and says. "Five hundred thousand dollars."

"Can anyone beat that?" The woman asks.

Someone in the front lifts his number and says. "Nine hundred thousand."

Vadim throws his number down and growled. "One million dollars and a donation of your choice."

The man in the front row shakes his head in disbelief. And I thank God for that.

"Going once. Going twice. Sold to 74960!"

Wait, what!
Vadim bought me.
But why?

I feel Yuri's breath on my neck when he unchains my wrists. "Now it begins, my sweet Jules. Let's hope you make it out alive. Well, that's if Vadim doesn't kill you before the game ends."

Game?

An hour later, I'm forced into a room and shoved to my knees. His boot hits my back and slams his foot down. I cried out in pain as his heel digs into my skin. My blood froze when I heard the shot and the man who kicked me to collapse to the floor.

It should scare me Vadim just killed a man. I could be next. It should make me sick. It doesn't. It only makes me crave his touch. Vadim tucked the gun inside the front of his pants and knelt to my level. He grasped the chain of my necklace and ripped it off.

His thick Russian accent murmured, "My sweet Angel, we meet again."

"Vadim…" I breathed out, "It's really you."

"Alexei," Vadim snapped, "Get the car ready. We're going home."

Home?

Vadim lifted me, cradling me his chest. I wrapped my arms around his neck and whispered. "Thank you for saving me again, Sir."

Vadim carried me away and met Alexei at the car. Vadim slipped into the car and slammed the door.

"Drive!" Vadim ordered Alexei.

Vadim cupped my jaw and narrowed his eyes when he saw the bruise on my cheek. He stroked it with his thumb and cursed under his breath. I leaned into his hand and moaned.

"Spread your legs. I want to see if I got what I paid for."

"W-what?" I stuttered.

"Spread your thighs, Angel. I want to see the goods."

And I do.
Because he owned me now.

"Hmm, that's a good girl." Vadim cooed, "Open for Daddy, my prized jewel." He spreads my pussy lips and slid a finger inside me. I moaned again. The effects of the drug make me arch my back.

"Netronutyy," he mused, "Pure, untouched, and all mine."

Chapter 2

Vadim

Fuck!

It was taking everything in my power to hold back. All I wanted was to rip her innocence away from her. The last time I saw her was after I sent her away. I watched her beg and cry as Alexei escorted her out of the estate. The day after that, she was adopted. I convinced myself I did the right thing. That she would live a normal life.

Evidently not.

I could feel her arousal soaking my finger. However, I could also tell she was still a virgin. Which is why I stopped. I knew the motherfucker drugged her. That's another reason I won't take her. If I was going to fuck her, she would remember it.

Alexei glanced at the mirror, throwing me a warning glance. He was telling me to let it go. That I was out of my mind. I rolled up the partition and pressed my lips to her neck. I reluctantly withdrew my finger and whispered to her. "We need to go over the rules. I've added a few more."

"Rule number one is the same as before. You remember, yes?"

"Yes, Sir. Always do as you say."

"Rule number two. If you disobey, you will be punished as I see fit."

"What's rule number three?"

"Never look at another man. Always be loyal to me. Failure to do so, see rule number two."

Her blue eyes widened when I sucked her juices from my finger. Her cheeks flushed crimson, averting her gaze. I clenched her robe and jerked her forward. She let out a squeak when I leaned closer to her neck. I inhaled and moaned. "You still smell so sweet, Angel."

She tried to look away, but I growled in frustration.

"Never look away from me." I ordered, gripping her jaw.

I forced her head up and watched fear grip her.

"Y-yes, Sir," she stuttered.

"I know you're a virgin, but have you ever pleasured a man?"

She swallowed hard and nodded.

"Who was it?" I practically growl.

She shook her head, squeezing her eyes shut.

"Are you telling me no, girl?"

Her eyes snapped open, her chest heaves in panic.

"No, Sir. It was…" she hesitates, "You'll be angry."

"I won't. Give me a name."

"Mama made me entertain him… Yuri."

Tears streamed down her cheeks.

"Angel, I'm not angry with you."

Only with Yuri.
And the foster parents.

I rolled down the partition and leaned forward to whisper to Alexei. "Drop us off at the estate. I want the city combed for the parents. Bring them to me. Alive."

He nodded.

Alexei dropped us at the estate and took off straight after. I took off my jacket and draped it over her. I helped her inside and met Regina at the door. "Take Miss Jules to her room and prepare her a bath."

"Is that…"

"Please, Regina. I need you to clean her up." I tell her.

"Sir, thank you." She whispered.

Oh sweetheart, I didn't save you.

I just tossed you in the Devil's Lair.

Just because I didn't want anyone else to have you.

"Go with Regina so you can get some proper clothes."

Not that she would be wearing any much.

Regina eyes me suspiciously but takes Jewel to her room. She may have changed her name to Jules, but she would always be Jewel to me. I loosened my tie and made my way to my bedroom.

"What the hell are you doing, Vadim?" I whispered to myself.

"That's what I'd like to know." I heard my brother say.

I turned and glared. "Oh, it's you."

He grinned, "Were those nipple rings on that girl you brought home?"

"You best keep your eyes off my property." I hissed.

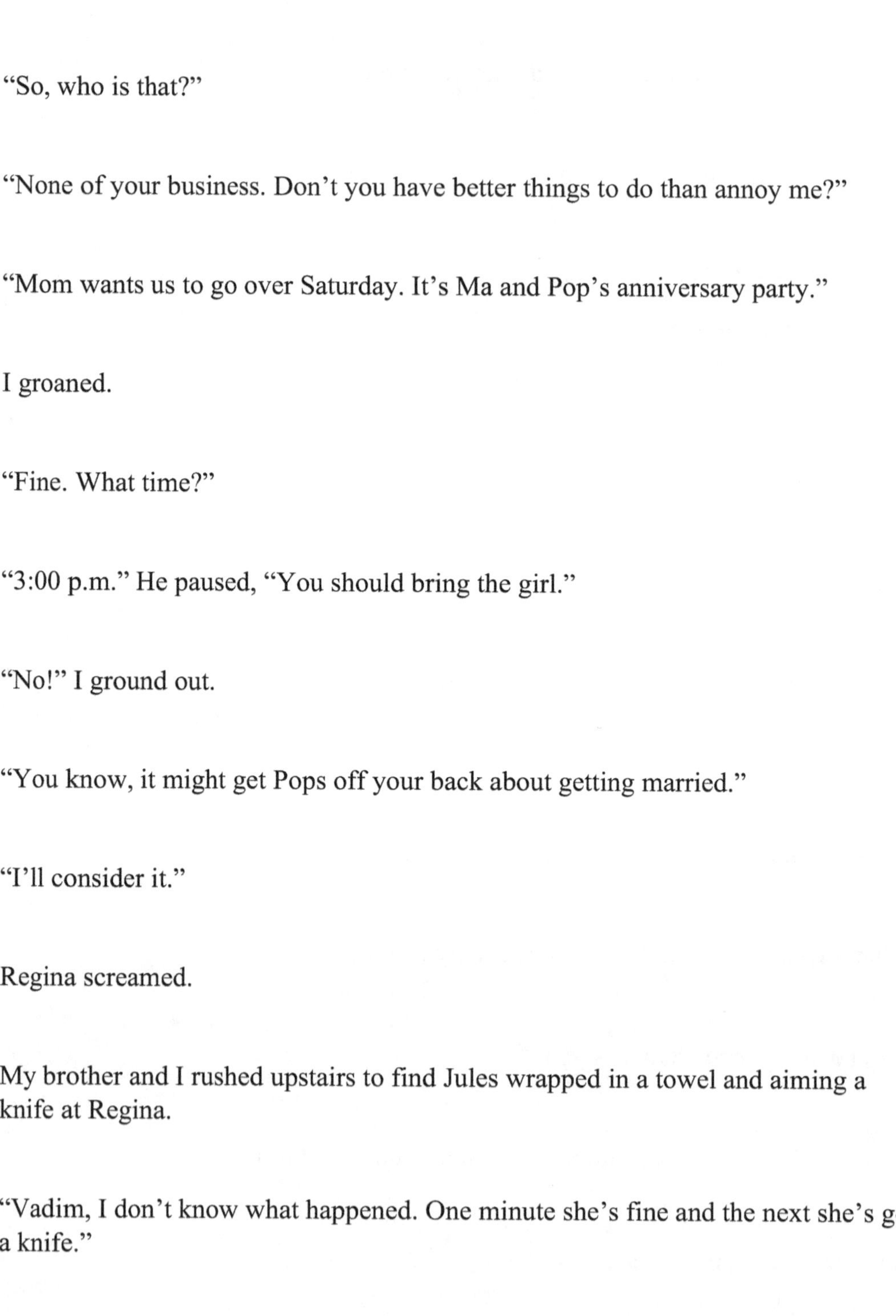

"So, who is that?"

"None of your business. Don't you have better things to do than annoy me?"

"Mom wants us to go over Saturday. It's Ma and Pop's anniversary party."

I groaned.

"Fine. What time?"

"3:00 p.m." He paused, "You should bring the girl."

"No!" I ground out.

"You know, it might get Pops off your back about getting married."

"I'll consider it."

Regina screamed.

My brother and I rushed upstairs to find Jules wrapped in a towel and aiming a knife at Regina.

"Vadim, I don't know what happened. One minute she's fine and the next she's got a knife."

"It's okay, Regina. Go downstairs and start dinner."

My brother lingers, but I shake my head.

"You go too. I got this."

"But…"

"Go. Now!" I growled.

I held my hands up in surrender and slowly make my way across the room. Jules holds the knife to her neck and hissed. "Don't come any closer."

"You and I both know you won't do it."

I take another step.
She takes one back.

"I-I'll do it." She threatened.

"Give me the knife, Angel."

I could take the knife at any moment. But it's not about power right now. It's about getting the feral kitten to trust me. Trust is the key.

Her eyes dart around the room as if looking for a way out. She moves to the left. So do I. Then, to the right. I'm quicker. She drops her arm and admits defeat. Just as I take a step closer, she aims it at my chest. I take another step and wrap my hand around her wrists. I lean into the knife and dare her. "Do it, Angel."

Her lips quivered and closed her eyes. I take the knife from her and toss it to the floor.

"D-don't hurt me, Sir."

"You know me, Angel. You know I won't hurt you… not unless I'm punishing you."

"I-I'm sorry," she whispered.

"Why did you try to hurt Regina?"

"She wanted to touch me. She said she wanted to apply cream to my piercings."

"You have to put medicine on them if you want them to heal."

"Sir, will you do it?"

Fuck me.

"Maybe…"

"I only trust you, Sir. Please."

"Okay," I sighed, "I'll have to touch you."

"It's okay, I trust you."

"You shouldn't, Angel," I murmured. "I'm a very bad man"

"But you saved me… twice."

No, Angel.
I didn't save you.
I took you for myself.
Because I'm a greedy man.

"Take off the towel and lie down on the bed."

She does and fuck me, all I want to do is spread her thighs and devour her. Eat her pussy until she passes out from exhaustion.

I grabbed the cream and sat at the edge of the bed. I unscrewed the cap and squeezed the tube. I set the tube down and rubbed my hands together. I gently rub her breasts and groan. Jewel moans and whispered. "Thank you, Sir. It feels so good."

"Malyshka," I groaned, "You have no idea how bad I want you."

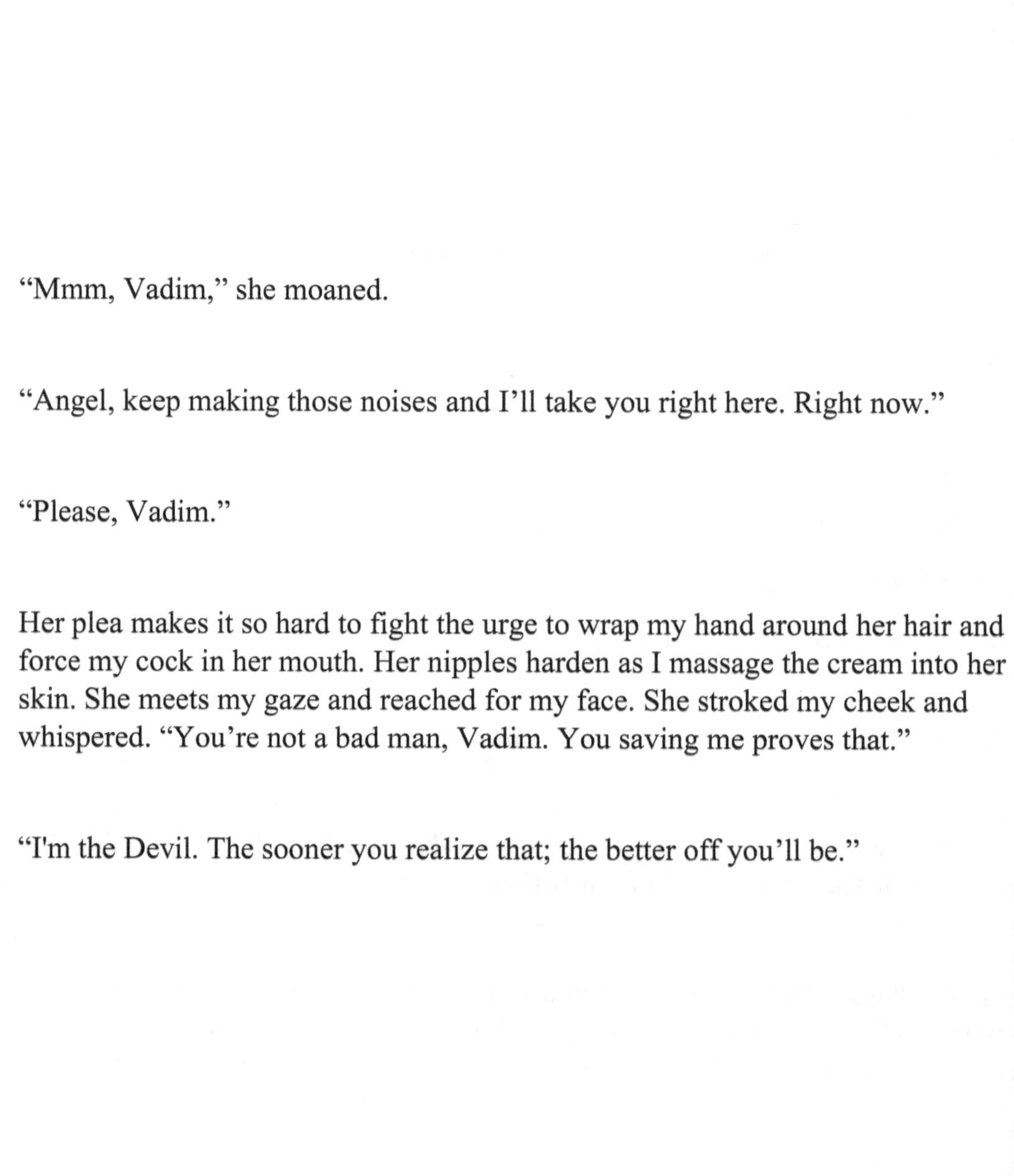

"Mmm, Vadim," she moaned.

"Angel, keep making those noises and I'll take you right here. Right now."

"Please, Vadim."

Her plea makes it so hard to fight the urge to wrap my hand around her hair and force my cock in her mouth. Her nipples harden as I massage the cream into her skin. She meets my gaze and reached for my face. She stroked my cheek and whispered. "You're not a bad man, Vadim. You saving me proves that."

"I'm the Devil. The sooner you realize that; the better off you'll be."

Chapter 3

Jules

"I'm the Devil. The sooner you realize that; the better off you'll be."

"But…"

"No, Angel," he chuckled darkly, "I'm as bad as they come. You'll find out soon enough."

Deep down I knew what kind of man Vadim was. He's a rabid beast. Ruthless. Dominant. Mafia. But still a sexy beast.

"I don't care that you've killed or tortured. You're a good man, Vadim."

He penetrated me with his fiery gaze and wrapped his hand firmly around my neck. I clawed at his wrist with both hands as I gasped for air.

"Vadim…" I whimpered. "Please."

"Angel, you have no idea how powerful I am. If I really wanted to, I could take your tight virgin cunt. There wouldn't be anything you could do about it either. I take what I want when I want."

Vadim's threat and tenebrous stare makes me rethink my assessment of him. Instead of being quiet, I whisper. "Then what are you waiting for? Take what you paid for."

This side of Vadim excites me. He sets my body on fire. There's nothing stopping him from taking me.

So, what's he waiting for?

"Spread your thighs." He snaps.

I have no choice but to obey.

I bit my lip as he released my neck. Nerves twist as he brings his hand to my cheek and murmured. "Open up for me, Malyshka."

I part my lips and moan when his thumb traces my mouth. I can feel his hardened member brush against my pussy lips through his pants as he pressed up against me. The bittersweet taste hits my tongue when he forces his thumb in my mouth. He cursed under his breath as he slides it in and out like it's his cock. A small whimper escaped my lips when he retracted his thumb. I was desperate for more. Obviously, the drugs still in my system. I blame the drugs, but that's not why I'm acting like a whore. No. I craved Vadim in ways I'd never craved anything before. One touch from Vadim wouldn't be enough to satisfy my hunger. I needed more. Wanted more.

"Please, Vadim," I whimpered, "Please, don't stop touching me."

"Oh, my little Jewel, I'm just getting started."

"What are you…"

Vadim crushed his lips against mine and kissed me hard. He groaned as he claimed my mouth furiously. His tongue skimmed my bottom lip and invaded me. And my body surrendered to him no accord. I submitted willingly.

"Please, Master…"

"Malyshka," he growled, "If I don't stop now, I'll break you."

"How can you break something that's already been broken? I'm damaged beyond repair. Tainted."

Vadim growled; his eyes flared in anger. He tipped his head to the side and brushed his lips against my ear. I shuddered when he hissed lowly. "You're not broken… not yet."

His promise leaves me breathless as he parts my slit and slid his middle finger inside. He stretched my walls and hums in approval. "Hmm, why is my Virgin so wet?"

His promise rings in my head.

"You're not broken… not yet."

"Break me," I whispered.

"Not yet, Malyshka, but soon."

I arched my back when he speeds his thrusts and smiled in satisfaction.

"Make me cum, Vadim."

Vadim's lips curve as he retracted his finger.

No!

"Fuuck!" I cried out, "P-please, keep going."

His eyes narrow into slits and he says. "You will cum, but only when I say so."

"Vadim…"

"No! You're not ready yet."

"I'm ready." I argued.

"No," He chuckled and shook his head. "You, my little Angel, are not ready to cum."

"Boss? I have news to report." I hear one of his men say through the door.

"Stay here, I'll be right back." He kissed my forehead, "You can touch yourself, but don't cum."

Vadim pulled away and stepped out of the room. I closed my eyes and let my fingers dance between my thighs. I opened my slit with two fingers and bucked my hips. Sliding my digits over my button, I moaned loudly. Even though the piercing throbbed, I kept circling my clit. The pain of needing to cum was way worse than the metal that pierced my tender flesh.

My eyelids fluttered and my body trembled when my breaths quickened. "Mmm, feels so good."

 Through my blurry vision, I see Vadim step back into the room. He locked onto me, his eyes darkening with each step. His lips twitched as he discarded his suit jacket dropped it to the floor. Another step. Another piece of his clothes gone. This time, his tie.

"Mmm, Vadim," I whimpered, my fingers trembling as my ass comes off the mattress.

Vadim untucked his shirt and began to unbutton his shirt. Tears leaked from the corner of my eyes, a tightness forming in the lower region. I paused my movements only to hear him demand. "Keep going, baby girl."

I raised my head and mewled. "Vadim, please… make it go away."

Vadim's shirt falls off his broad shoulders and down his massive arms. He's nothing but perfection under his suit. Muscles and tattoos. It's everything that makes my pussy purr. He eased onto the bed and slithered up my body. His breath hits my skin when he lightly blows on my nipples.

"Vadim, touch me… please." I whispered through harsh breaths.

"Beg, Malyshka. Tell me how bad you want me."

"I-I… please, I need to… I'm begging you."

"Hmm," he mused, "I love hearing you beg for it. It makes my dick so goddamn hard hearing those sexy noises. Do you have any idea how hard it is to hold myself back?"

"Taste me, Vadim."

"Taste you? Tell me where you want me to taste your sweetness."

"My pussy, Vadim."

Vadim spread my slit and stroked my clit. Everything seemed to go by in a blur when he rubbed my tenderness faster. The throb in my sex made me cry out in ecstasy.

"Yes, Vadim!"

"That's a good girl. Tell me how bad you want to cum."

"So bad," I whimpered.

I was under his control as he kissed my lips. Completely and utterly at his mercy.

"Cum, Malyshka. Get your pussy nice and wet for Daddy."

"Vadim…"

"That's not my name!" Vadim growled.

"What…"

Vadim cupped my jaw and hissed. "You will call me Daddy."

"I'm not…"

Smack!

"Say it." He smacked my thigh. "Daddy."

"Please, Daddy."

"That's better. Now, it's my turn. You are going to open that pretty mouth and watch me fuck your face."

"No!" I blurted out.

"Are you telling me no?"

"I-I… Vadim…"

"You will obey me at all times," Vadim gripped my jaw and squeezed hard. "You will do exactly as I tell you or receive a punishment."

"Fuck you!" I growled.

What am I doing?

Where's this confidence coming from?

He tightened his grip, causing me to cry out in pain. "If I want you to get on your knees in front of my men and suck my dick, you fucking will. You. Are. Mine."

"Do you want your punishment now or later, Malyshka?"

"Now, Daddy."

"Turn over and present your ass."

I didn't have time to turn over because Vadim hauled me over his lap.

"I'll be gentle since it's your first time. I'm going to give you five spanks for disobedience and count each one."

Smack!

"One, Sir," I moaned.

Vadim smoothed his palm over my ass to soothe the sting. He brought it down on my left ass cheek. This time, harder than last time. Tears rolled down my face.

"T-two, Sir."

Another smack.

"Three, Sir," I moaned.

Two more swift spanks. One on each cheek.

"Four, five, Sir."

"Spread your legs and let me see how wet you are." Vadim demanded.

His fingers probed my slit and rubbed circles on my clit.

"Good girl," he praised, "Does my Angel wish to cum?"

"Please, Daddy," I begged.

I arched my back and rocked my hips. Vadim slid one finger inside me and stroked my clit with the pad of his thumb. Vadim grabbed a fistful of my hair and yanked my head back. He leaned down and whispered in my ear. "Cum, Angel. Cum on my finger.

"Ooh, Daddy," I cried out, "I'm going to…"

"Cum!" he growled.

"Oh god, I am! Fuck, Daddy."

I felt my pussy clamp around his finger and coat him with my juices. Even after I came, he kept pumping his finger. He added another and groaned. "So wet, Angel. Tight and all mine."

"Please, Vadim."

Vadim retracted his finger and flipped me over on my back. He brought his glistening finger to my mouth and commanded me. "Suck, Angel."

I parted my lips and sucked seductively. Vadim cursed in Russian and forced more of his digit into my mouth. I didn't think I would like to taste myself, but I do. It's sweet with a hint of bitterness.

He retracted his finger, "Now, Angel, down on your knees."

"W-what?" I stuttered.

"Down on your knees."

"Boss?" I hear Alexei question Vadim, "Is now a bad time?"

"No, come in and have a drink with me."

I widened my eyes when Vadim shoved me to the floor and unzipped his pants. "Suck."

"But…"

"I told you, Angel. You will do as I say. And right now, you will suck me off in front of Alexei."

Chapter 4

Vadim

Alexei entered the room and averted his gaze from the Angel on her knees. I found the back of her neck and eased my hardened member in her mouth. I leaned my head back and groaned. "Fuck, Angel."

"Boss?" Alexei asked.

"Come have a drink." I said.

Alexei nervously poured Vodka into two glasses, trying not to glance at Jules.

"It's okay, Alexei. You can look."

Alexei downed the contents of his glass and slammed it down on the counter. Alexei stayed behind the counter, obviously to hide the fact he was aroused. I patted the spot next to me and said. "Sit with me."

He stepped around the counter and sat next to me. Jules bobbed her head, moaning softly. Alexei swallowed hard and covered his erection. I chuckled and wrapped my arm around his shoulder. "She's beautiful, yes?"

"Yes, boss," he whispered. "Very beautiful."

"Would you like a taste?" I asked.

He shook his head.

"It's okay. Since you're my number one man, I'll let you join us."

I pulled out of Jules's mouth and whispered to Alexei. "What would you like her to do?"

"Suck me off," he rasped.

"Angel, how would you like to be shared?"

Her eyes widen when Alexei licked his lips.

"Vadim, I-I…"

"Alexei is going to take out his cock and slide it into your mouth. You will suck him off."

"Vadim…" Jules whispered.

"And he's going to cum in your mouth. You will swallow it and thank him for feeding you."

"Yes, Daddy."

"Good girl," I murmured, "Slide over and serve him."

Alexei unbuttoned his pants and unzipped them, sliding them down. His cock stood proud as it popped out from his pants. Jules slid over and wrapped her fingers around the shaft. She ran her tongue around the head as she looked him in the eyes.

"God," Alexei moaned, "khoroshaya devushka."

I stroked her cheek and said, "She's a very good girl."

"Shit, Malyshka," Alexei thrust his hips, "Suck faster."

It would be so easy to get behind her and take what I paid for. But I won't. Not yet. Jules isn't ready to take me in her pussy. However, I can pleasure her in other ways.

"How close are you to coming, Alexei?" I asked.

"S-so close, boss." He whispered.

"Cum, Alexei. Fill her mouth with your cum."

"Fuuck, yes! Going to cum now."

Jules whimpered when I slid behind her and pulled her arms behind her back. I held her wrists with one hand and reached between her thighs. I pressed my lips to her neck and groaned against her. "Be a good a khoroshaya devushka for Daddy and swallow every drop."

Alexei closed his eyes and lolled his head back. His hips bucked, filling her mouth with his cum. Her soft moans did nothing but turn me on even more. "God, you look so sexy with a cock in your mouth."

Alexei pulled out of her mouth, his member going soft.

"Thank you for feeding me, Alexei," Jules whispered.

"You're welcome, sweetheart."

Alexei tucked his cock in his pants and zipped them back up, buttoning it.

"You're such a good girl," I said delving into her wetness.

"Please, Vadim," Jules moaned.

"Tonight, is the night, baby girl. I'm going to take your pussy for the first time. And guess what?"

She shook her.

"Alexei is going to watch you be taken by me."

"Is he going to join us?" Jules asked.

"Maybe, but that's entirely up to him."

I pumped my fingers and hear Jules' harsh breaths. Her moans fill the room and fuck me, tonight can't come soon enough.

"Isn't she beautiful, Alexei?" I asked.

"Da, boss," Alexei whispered huskily. "Very beautiful."

Alexei shifted in his seat uncomfortably. He's obviously aroused again, despite just getting off to her.

"Jules," I murmured softly, "Do you wish to cum?"

"Yes, Sir," she moaned out loudly.

I held her wrists tighter and retracted my fingers from her wetness and smirked when she let out a strangled moan.

"P-please, don't stop."

I pressed my fingers against her clit and worked slow circles around it. Alexei leaned forward and cupped the side of her face. He lifted his eyes and whispered. "Boss, may I..."

"Kiss her, Alexei." I said, applying more pressure to her clit.

Alexei closed the space, crushing his mouth against hers. I should be jealous of another man touching Jules. However, that's not the case. Seeing my second-in-command make out with Jules has me on fire. No. Not angry, but burning with desire. All I want to do is spread her out and take her. Deep. Hard. Fuck her real good. Devirginize my little Jewel. And after, watch Alexei make her cum again on his dick.

Alexei groaned, taking one hand off her cheek to slide it down to his crotch. For someone who was so against buying Luciano's sister, he sure is keen on kissing her. I didn't force his hand. I merely invited him to the party. He's the one who asked to indulge in the forbidden fruit.

My strokes in Jules become quicker, more fierce. I know she's close because of her labored breaths.

"You may cum, Malyshka."

I slid a finger into her wetness and move my thumb over her clit. She gasped and arched her back.

"I'm coming, Sir," she moaned in Alexei's mouth.

Alexei tears his lips away and leans back to watch Jules convulse against my body. Her pussy clenched around my finger, making a slow smirk spread across my face. Alexei whispered Russian profanities under his breath as Jules cums hard. She cries out, falling limp against my chest. I feel Jules juices slick on my finger, a sloshing sound in the air.

"Oh, please, Sir, d-don't stop!" Jules cried out.

"Let it go, Malyshka," I coaxed her.

She does. And it's the most beautiful thing I've ever seen. My eyes travel to Alexei and I smirk. He's stroking himself through his pants. His head falls back, and he parts his lips, his breaths erratic. I'll be back for him, but first, I need to put Jules to bed.

I took Jules limp body in my arms, holding her to my chest. Carrying her across the room, I laid her gently onto the bed and covered her naked body with a blanket. I smiled down at her when I heard her let out a satisfied sigh and whisper. "Thank you, Sir."

"Rest, baby girl," I murmured, leaning down and kissed her forehead.

Now for Alexei.

He deserves a reward for showing so much restraint.

I walked across the room, careful not to alert Alexei. Now, he's got his pants undone. He's breathing heavily as he pumps his cock in his fist. I slide next to him and put my arm around his shoulders.

"B-boss?"

"Shh, let me help you. You want to cum, yes?"

My free hand covered his and help him stroke his dick. His head falls back on my arm and groans. "Boss, what are…"

I crush my lips against his mouth and make him stroke himself faster. I love pussy, but nothing turns me on more than my second-in-command. He moaned when I slide my tongue into his mouth.

"F-fuck, boss," he whispered. "I'm going…"

I pulled away from his lips and demanded. "Cum, Alexei."

Cum shoots out as he bucks his hips against my hand.

"Vadim, I'm coming… feels so good, boss."

Alexei's body jerked as the last of his cum shot out. When he's caught his breath, his eyes widen when he realizes how close our bodies are. "Relax, Alexei, it's just us right now."

"I'm sorry, boss. I-I…"

"Just go with it, Alexei." I whispered, crushing my mouth against his lips once again.

I felt Alexei stiffen when I pulled him closer.

"Relax, it's just us."

"B-boss?"

"Shh, submit to me."

Alexei pulled away and glanced across the room. Jules was curled up on the bed sleeping.

"Do you want to watch me pop her cherry?" I asked.

I knew he did.
Just needed to hear him say the words.

"Yes," he whispered.

Alexei turned away from me as I watched him squirm in his seat.

"Would you like to join me when I fuck her for the first time?"

"Yes, boss."

"Good, I want you to get our girl nice and wet after you wash off. Get Jules ready to take my dick in her unused pussy."

Alexei went to tuck himself back into his pants, but I grabbed his wrist. "Take off your clothes and shower."

Alexei hesitated at first but stripped his clothes off. He stepped into the bathroom, leaving the door ajar. This gives me the perfect opportunity to grab a few things.

A blindfold.

Rope.

Ball gag.

Vibrator.

And my personal favorite.

Butt plug.

I took off my shoes and my jacket. I laid it on the couch and unbuttoned my shirt. Stripping out of my pants, I sat on the edge of the bed and glanced towards the bathroom. I could see Alexei's bare ass through the glass as he showered. I could go in there and press my body against him. Shove him against the wall. Take him. But I decided to wait.

"Soon, Alexei. But not yet." I whispered to myself.

I wanted to hear him say it.

Wanted to hear him beg me to fuck him.

I would.

But not yet.

Soon though… very, very soon.

I saw Alexei step out of the bathroom with a towel wrapped around his waist. He eyed the toys I had laid out on the bed and bit his lip.

"Drop the towel," I demanded.

Alexei dropped the towel and cupped his private area to hide his erection.

I chuckled softly at that.

"Now, get on the bed and get her wet."

Alexei pulled the covers off Jules and climbed onto the bed. He forced her thighs apart and kissed her inner thigh. I stood up and stepped behind Alexei. My hands found his hips and ground into him. "Fuck her with your tongue."

Jules parted her lips, her blue eyes fluttering open. She widened her eyes, shocked that it wasn't me that was between her thighs. She moaned when Alexei palmed one of her breasts. I leaned over Alexei and whispered. "Good boy."

Alexei groaned when he felt how hard I was. Jules threaded her fingers in Alexei's hair and bucked her hips. She looked good like this. Completely at our mercy. I pulled away from Alexei and picked up the rope. I stood over Jules and grinned. "Hands up, Malyshka."

She held onto the headboard and swallowed hard. She looked frightened.

"Don't be scared, little one. Do you trust me?"

"Yes, Sir."

She shouldn't.

Lord help me, she shouldn't.

But she does.

Perfectly submissive to me.

I wrapped the rope around her wrists and tied it in a knot. I tugged on it and smile down at her. Her blue eyes dilated as she began to get closer to a release. I didn't know it was because Alexei's tongue was doing wonders or if tying her up did her in. Either way, she was going to cum on his face. I climbed onto the bed and caressed her cheek. "Cum, Maylyshka. I want you to drench Alexei's face."

She does and it's glorious.

"Is she wet, Alexei?"

"Yes," he whispered as he pulled away from her.

"Good. I want you to take my place. It's time for me to take what I paid for."

I glanced at Jules and asked. "Do you want me to fuck you while Alexei watches?"

"Yes," she whispered.

Chapter 5

Alexei

I took Vadim's place next to Jules and watched my boss. He tugged his boxer briefs and knelt on the bed. I couldn't stop thinking about Vadim. He stroked himself and glanced at me. A slow, devious grin crept across his lips.

"Come here, Alexei."

I crawled to him and stared into his eyes. He sucked me in with his hardened eyes and demanded. "Get down there and get my dick wet."

I took him in my mouth and sucked greedily. So many nights I've wanted to do this. And so many nights I got off as I whispered Vadim's name. I love a pussy, but I also swing the other way too.

"Go deeper," he growled.

I take him deeper and gag when the tip hits the back of my throat. Vadim cursed under his breath and ran his hand down my back. He finds the back of my neck and thrusts his hips. I reached down between my legs and stroked myself.

Vadim threaded his fingers in my hair and took it in his fist, jerking my head back. "Lie down next to her and kiss her."

"Yes, boss." I whispered.

I laid next to Jules and turn my head to face her. Her blue eyes sear into me as I lean into her. I kiss her gently as Vadim eases his cock inside her. She whimpered into my mouth as he slides a little more in. Tears leak from the corner of her eyes, thrashing against the rope.

"Relax, baby girl." I hear Vadim tell her. "It's almost in."

When he's all the way in, he groaned. "Fuck, Maylyshka."

I can tell Vadim is holding back, so he doesn't hurt her. I keep kissing her and palm her left breast. I brushed my thumb over her pierced nipple and hear her whimpers turn into moans of pleasure.

"Alexei, stroke her clit."

I pulled away from her lips and scoot over to her hips. I pressed two fingers to her swollen clit and stroked her. She bucked her hips and cries out. Her thighs trembled as Vadim pumps his cock in and out. Her fists clenched and moaned when Vadim fucked her harder. Now that she's gotten used to Vadim's cock, he's going harder.

"Damn, baby girl, I'm not going to last too much longer. You're. Too. Tight."

"I'm going to cum," she whimpered.

"Cum, baby girl." He growled.

Vadim pulled out and stroked himself as he came on her stomach. Thick ropes of his cum shot on her skin, marking her as his.

"Clean her, Alexei. I know you're just dying to have a taste."

My tongue runs over her belly and licks the remnants of his cum. The taste is bitter, but so good. I love how he tastes. Bitter and sweet. My balls ache from needing to cum. I finish licking the last of his cum and meet his gaze. He breaks his stare to look down between my legs. "Go sit on the couch, Alexei, do you wish to cum?"

"Yes, boss."

"Lie down on your back while I untie Jules. She's going to take care of your needs."

I laid on my back and stroked my cock. The veins on my length were visible and my balls hurt. They hurt so damn bad. Vadim helped Jules straddle my thighs and whispered to her. "Jerk Alexei off. He needs to be taken care of."

Jules wrapped both hands around my length and stroked me. I closed my eyes and let out a strangled moan. Her hands felt good, but her pussy would be better. Or her ass.

"Such a good girl," he murmured,

I mumbled under my breath and sucked in a breath. Tingles ran through me when I felt Vadim's fingers take one of my nipples between his finger and thumb.

"Oh, fuck," I groaned.

"Put your mouth on him, baby girl. Suck him off."

I opened my eyes and hissed. "Fuck, Malyshka. Almost. There."

I clenched the sheets and my hips jerked as I came in her mouth and holy shit, it felt so good. My body relaxed and a sigh escaped my lips as she swallowed my cum. Vadim brought his finger to the corner of her mouth and wipes the small drop of my cum off of her. He puts his finger in his mouth, sucking it off and moaned in approval. "Delicious."

I can't help but blush at the sight of my boss tasting me.

Secretly, I want him to bend me over the bed and fuck my ass.

I can't help but feel jealous that Jules got fucked by him.

And the way Vadim is looking at me, he knows exactly what I'm thinking about.

"Don't worry, Alexei. You're next."

Chapter 6

Jules

I never thought having two men pleasure me could be this intense. It was so much more. The way Alexei's tongue felt on me had me feel like I was going to explode. And watching Vadim and Alexei together was the hottest thing I'd ever seen.

I ached between my legs, but it was a good ache. Vadim took me gentle at first. Then, something snapped in Vadim. His eyes darkened, a storm was brewing in them. He took what he wanted. And I gladly gave it to him.

"Malyshka, give me a kiss." Vadim demanded.

I kissed him softly, but he had other plans. He swallowed me and consumed me. He drank me in and deepened the kiss. The darkness in his eyes told me he wasn't done with me yet. And just like that, I'm ready to be taken by this beast of a man.

Vadim pulled away and crushed his lips against Alexei's mouth. Doing the same thing to him. Only this time, the kiss was ravenous. Like he couldn't get enough of his second-in-command. Vadim tore his mouth away from Alexei and commanded him. "Now, you kiss her. Make love to her mouth, Alexei."

Alexei leaned over and covered my mouth with his. Vadim skimmed his fingers over my hips and groaned. "Yeah, that's it, baby girl. Submit to him. Give him your all."

"Alexei," I moaned.

"Good girl," Vadim praised me as he took my breasts in his hands and squeezed. I gasped when he shoved them together. His thumbs brushed my tightened nipples and cursed under his breath.

I didn't know what he was saying, but it sounded hot coming out of his mouth. Alexei pulled away from me and whispered to me. "Do you want more, my little Jewel?"

I nodded.

I craved each one like crazy.

Vadim saved me.

No.

He saved me once.

And then, when I saw him again… he bought me.

Now, he owns me.

Alexei did too.

Vadim was nothing like Yuri. Sure, he's dark and dangerous, but with me he's gentle when he needs to be. And when I need him to be the beast, he is. His wolf scratches through the surface and takes me. Fierce. Hard. Passionate.

Alexei on the other hand, he's here with us because his boss wants him to be. While Alexei is gentle, Vadim is rough. And me? I'm their shiny new toy. They call me their little jewel. Baby girl. Good girl. And I am. I'll be anything they want me to be as long as I can have them both.

"Go get the shower ready, Alexei. We need to clean our little Jules up."

Alexei leaves to get the water warmed up and I'm left with Vadim. He traced my cheek and murmured, "I didn't hurt you, did I?"

"No, Sir. Everything was perfect."

"Good. Because I'm nowhere near done with you."

Vadim picked me up gently and held me to his chest. He kissed my temple and whispered in my ear. "Let's get you cleaned up, Malyshka."

Vadim stepped into the bathroom and set me on the sink. He glanced back to the shower and curved his lips. Alexei was standing under the water with his eyes closed. He tilted his head back as he stroked himself. Vadim met my flushed state and smirked. "Seems like Alexei needs some more attention."

I licked my lips and breathed out, "Yes, it seems like he does."

"Go inside and give him a hand. I'll be right behind you."

I slid off the sink, but Vadim wrapped his hand around my wrist. "Make him feel real good, Malyshka."

"Yes, Sir."

I opened the door to the shower and stepped inside. I pressed one hand onto Alexei's chest and one around his hand that was stroking his cock. His eyes snapped open, a panic flashing through them.

"It's okay, Alexei. Vadim is right behind me."

"Fuck, baby girl," he swore, "You're so addictive."

"She is," Vadim chimed. "Our little Jules has become quite the obsession."

I helped Alexei stroke his length and pressed my lips to his neck. Vadim wrapped his arms around my waist and kissed my shoulder. His mouth moved upward, making his way to the side of my neck.

"Vadim," Alexei groaned, "I've dreamed of this for so long."

"Oh yeah?" Vadim asked.

"Oh yeah, I've jacked off so many nights when I imagined you fucking my ass."

"That changes tonight."

Alexei froze mid-stroke.

"It changes tonight because tonight that fantasy becomes a reality. I'm going to bend you over my bed and fuck you. Hard. Fast. I'm going to obliterate you."

"Oh, fuck… I'm going to cum!"

I massaged Alexei's nipple as I sucked on his neck. And Alexei came on me for the second time tonight. His hot cum splashed against me and painted my flesh. I was marked once again. Vadim trailed his lips against my neck until his mouth was next to my ear. "Would you like to watch me fuck Alexei while he eats your pussy as a reward for being such a loyal soldier to me?"

"Yes, Sir," I whispered.

"Does it turn you on to see Alexei and myself together?"

"So much, Sir," I replied.

Alexei let out one more grunt and fell back against the tile, relaxing against me. Vadim took this chance to push me under the water. The hot water warmed my body as Vadim washed Alexei's cum off me.

"Fuck me, Malyshka." Vadim swore, "I can't wait to see Alexei's face buried between your thighs while I fuck him."

Vadim circled his arm around my waist and whispered softly. "Do you think you can handle us at the same time?"

I moaned when he cupped my pussy and squeezed.

Alexei stepped forward and curved his lips. I was once again sandwiched between the two of them. Just as Alexei was about to close the gap and kiss me, I heard a knock on the door. Vadim groaned and kissed my temple. "I'll be right back. I want you and Alexei to get out and dry off. Alexei, start warming her up for us."

"Boss?" he questioned.

"I'm still going to fuck you, Alexei. Just as soon as we take her at the same time."

Alexei and I stepped out of the shower and dried off. I dropped the towel on the floor and started to turn the knob. Alexei covered my hand and whispered. "Let me make sure it's clear before we go in there."

"Alexei…"

"This isn't up for discussion, baby girl."

I turned to Alexei and nodded. I knew better than to argue. Alexei cracked the door open and nodded back to me. He took me by the wrist and led me to the end of the bed. My body was pushed down until I was on my hands and knees. "Face down, ass up with your thighs spread."

"W-what are you going to do?" I stuttered.

Alexei leaned over me and whispered in my ear, "I'm going to get you ready for the boss to take your ass. By doing that, I need to insert a butt plug to stretch you out for him."

A whimper escaped my lips when I felt cool liquid was squeezed on my ass hole. Alexei spread it around and slid his finger inside. I moaned when he slid in more up to his knuckles. It burned, but it brought an excitement inside me. He pumped his finger a few times and withdrew it. Cool metal was then pressed against me and pushed inside. He slowly pushed more of it into me and groaned. I felt my heartbeat pick up when he patted the plug with his hand and murmur. "And this is why we call you our little jewel. Vadim had this one special made for you to complete your piercings."

I tried to turn over but Alexei held me in place by the hips. "Keep this position, baby girl. I have a few more things to add."

Chapter 7

Vadim

Nothing pissed me off more than one of my men pulling me away from Jules and Alexei. Just when I was about to take them to my bed, I was interrupted. Someone better be dying or caught those responsible for hurting Jules.

"Well?" I asked, aggravation in my voice.

"B-boss, we've captured the mother."

"And the father?"

"H-he got away, Sir."

"Go tell Arianna to prepare the room for interrogation."

Saveli, an enforcer for me, clenched his jaw when I mentioned the young girl, I appointed him to train. "She is not ready for that."

"Saveli, I gave you one month to train her. She should be ready."

"Boss, she has been… difficult." He grumbled.

"Then, show her who's in charge. If you can't do it, I can appoint another man. I'm sure my brother would be more than willing to take your place."

"No," he hissed, "I'll make sure Arianna knows her place."

"Good. Make sure the mother suffers, but do not kill her."

"But I thought you wanted…"

"The mother will die at my hands, but only when I think she has suffered enough. Not a second too soon."

"Of course, boss."

"Let everyone know, I'm not to be disturbed for the rest of the night. I will be busy."

Saveli bowed in respect and murmured. "As you wish, Sir."

I entered my bedroom and smiled at Alexei as he met my gaze. He kissed Jules neck as he caressed one of her breasts. I disrobed and made my way over to Alexei. He stiffened when I rested my hands on his hips. I leaned down and whispered. "Do you want this, Alexei?"

"Yes, boss. I've dreamed of this moment for so long."

"Get Jules on her back and chain her to the bed, wrists and ankles." I demanded.

I crossed my arms over my chest as I watched my second-in-command restrain Jules to the bed. She met my dark gaze and bit her lip. She wanted this as much as I did. At first, I wanted to take Jules at the same time with Alexei. However, after seeing Alexei's ass bent over, I had a better idea. Alexei would bend over and offer himself to me as he buried his face between Jules. But first, he would have to beg for it. And when I felt like he deserved it, I would fuck him in the ass.

"Bend over, Alexei." It wasn't a request. He knew it.

Alexei bent over prepared to take my cock, but I grabbed the back of his head and shoved his face down. Right between Jules' legs. "If you want me to fuck you, you will have to work for it."

I kept my hand at the back of Alexei's head and could hear him sucking on her pussy. I shifted my gaze to Jules and watched in delight when she closed her eyes.

"Keep your eyes open, Malyshka. I want to see your eyes when you cum on Alexei's tongue."

"I… please… I don't think I can cum anymore." She moaned.

"You will cum as many times as I want you to."

"P-please, Vadim!" she begged.

I smiled when she curled her hands into fists, gritting her teeth. This is what I wanted. Something inside me wanted her to talk back to me. Just so I could punish her. Her thighs trembled when I pushed Alexei's face deeper. She arched her back as her chest began to rise and fall rapidly. But still yet, she never gave me any attitude. And that disappointed me. I wanted her to. I took Alexei's hair in my fist and yanked back. He gasped as I forced him to meet my hard gaze.

"Beg me," I ordered. "I want to hear you beseech for me to fuck you."

"Please," Alexei pleaded as I positioned myself behind him.

"You can do better than that. I want to hear you beg for your boss to fuck you." I hissed.

"Please, fuck me," he whimpered.

I released his hair and ran my hand down his back. He groaned in response when I palmed his ass. I squeezed hard and leaned over him to whisper in his ear. "Tell me how many times you came in your room when you thought of me."

"So… so many times, boss." He rasped.

"And did you moan my name?"

"Yes, boss," he breathed out.

"And if I fuck you right now, will you do it again?" I was teasing. Of course, I was going to fuck him regardless. This was more for Jules than anything else. She loved watching me with Alexei. And I loved the way she writhed against the chains. She was desperate to touch us.

"Take the restraints off Jules' wrists. I want her to jerk you off when I fuck you."

The rattling of chains echoed through the room. As he released her. Sweat formed on her forehead as she sat up. She placed her hands flat on her thighs, waiting for my order. She wanted to touch Alexei. And the way Alexei was breathing, he knew it too. But still, they both waited patiently.

"Touch him, Malyshka."

I reached over and grabbed the bottle of lube, squeezing a generous amount on my cock. I tossed the bottle to the side and stroked myself to lubricate my length. I pressed the tip against his hole and pushed the head in. He let out a strangled moan and clenched his fists in the sheets. I wrapped my arm around his waist and thrust my hips forward. Jules stroked him as she kissed him. The sight was beautiful. Another thrust and I'm in. I could feel his muscles tighten around my cock as I pumped my cock in and out of him.

"Vadim, fuck me harder," he moaned against Jules.

Our bodies clashed together in sweet harmony. While there was a woman being tortured in my basement, I was making love with my second-in-command and my little jewel. I could smell the sex in the air as I continued to drive into Alexei harder. I pressed my cheek against his back and groaned. "You feel so good, Alexei."

I raised my head and shoved Alexei's face back down between her thighs. I buried his face and growled as I took Alexei from behind. I couldn't think when sex was this intense. And the way Alexei's ass felt, it wouldn't be the last time I take him. Perhaps, next time, I would allow Alexei to fuck her in the pussy while I take him from behind.

Chapter 8

Yuri

The plan was coming along perfectly. I set the trap and Vadim took the bait just like I knew he would. My little Jules would be responsible for his downfall. I glanced to the younger man and curved my lips. "Have you brought me news, my boy?"

"They've captured the mother just like you planned."

"Good."

"Now what?" he asked.

"Now, we wait."

"Wait for what?"

"We wait for the pieces to come together. Are you backing out of the plan?"

"N-no, of course not. I just…"

I wrapped my hand around his neck and shoved him against the wall. He grasped my wrists in attempt to break away, but I pulled my gun out and pressed it to his forehead. He widened his eyes and gasped.

"If you even think of betraying me, I'll end you, boy. I'll ask you once more, are your intentions to betray me?"

"N-no, I swear. You can trust me."

"Can I trust you will fetch my Jules when I tell you to?"

"Yes, Sir."

"Keep your end of the deal and I'll reward you. Betray me and you'll end up just like your brother."

I released him and patted his cheek. "You can trust me, father."

"Good."

I could tell he was angry, but business is business. The sooner I take down Vadim and Alexei, the sooner I become the new King. And maybe if Jules comes out of this alive, I'll make her my mistress to tend to my needs. If… she makes it out of this war alive.

Chapter 9

Vadim

I entered the basement and eyed Saveli. Arianna was currently laying punch after punch. I raised my brow to my enforcer and smirked. He glared and shook his head. He knew I was right. Arianna was ready for this. He just didn't want to admit it. I knew Saveli better than I know myself. And I knew one thing for sure. He feels something for the girl. She looks sweet on the outside, but don't let that fool you. She'll cut your throat and leave you to bleed out in a ditch.

"Arianna, stop for a moment. I want to talk to her." I commanded.

Arianna backed away and bowed her head as I stepped closer to the woman. "You broke your word. You and that bastard husband of yours."

"I-I'm sorry…"

"You promised she would be safe with you. I'm very disappointed Cora."

"Where is she?"

"With me, where she's safe. Now, tell me, where can I find that husband of yours?"

I nodded at Arianna when she didn't answer. Arianna pulled out a knife and stood behind her as she pressed the blade to her neck. Arianna leaned down and hissed, "Tell him!"

I-I… please, I do not know." She whispered.

"Better yet, tell me where I can find the one who bought her from you."

"It was… Yuri, the one who set up the auction. He owns everything. Brothels. Underground auctions. Everything."

I glanced at Saveli and narrowed my eyes. "Keep her alive… for now. She may become of some use after all."

"And Arianna, good work. You'll make a good addition to the family."

"No!" Saveli hissed.

"Stop treating me like a child, Saveli!" she growled. "I'm not a little girl anymore."

"Saveli, do I need to reassign Arianna to someone else?"

"No. Boss." Saveli hissed through gritted teeth.

"Good. I'll have my brother on standby just in case."

Cora sobbed quietly and whispered, "Just kill me."

"No. I want to have the satisfaction of knowing you suffered for your crimes. In fact, I want you to watch me torture your husband and kill him right before your eyes."

"No! Please, spare me. It was all him... it was his idea."

"Keep torturing her, Arianna."

"You're not going to stay for the show?" Arianna asked.

"No. I have to go out. My mother is expecting me for dinner tonight."

I returned to my bedroom and smiled when I saw Jules in the dress Alexei laid out. She looked beautiful in it. A soft, red dress that came down to her knees. Alexei straightened up when he saw me, but I shook my head. "Relax, Alexei."

Jules turned around and hugged herself. I took a few long strides and cupped her face, kissing her gently. "You look beautiful, Malyshka."

"Why did you make me get dressed up if it's just dinner?"

"Because it's not any ordinary dinner. I'm taking you to my mother's house."

"And Alexei?"

"He will accompany me as well."

"What if she doesn't like me?" I could see the wheels turning like it always does.

"She will adore you, Malyshka."

I placed another kiss to her lips and glanced over at Alexei. I could see that he was feeling left out, so I held my hand out to him. "Come, Alexei."

Alexei stood and walked towards me. I wrapped my arm around his waist and crushed my lips against his and murmured. "Shall we go?"

"Yes, boss."

The ride to my mother's house only took about an hour. Alexei parked the car and hurried to open the door for me. I exited the car and was met with my brother. He curved his lips when I wrapped my arm around her waist protectively.

"Mother is waiting for you in the kitchen."

I led Jules into the house and was met with my mother's bright green eyes. She rushed to Jules and hugged her. I could tell Jules was nervous, but played it off very well. Jules hugged her back as my mother whispered in her ear.

"Mother," I muttered. "That is enough."

"Hush, Vadim. Let me look at you, sweetheart." My mother pulled away and studied Jules' face. "You are quite the little gem. I can see why my son has taken a liking to you."

I groaned when my father and brother enter the kitchen. My father's eyes light up when my brother whispered something to him. He's scheming against me. I know it.

"And who is this?" My father's deep voice asked.

"Jules, this is my father… Boris Kaslov and this is my mother… Angelina Kaslov. It's their 50th anniversary today."

"It's nice to meet you," Jules whispered.

"Vadim," my father cleared his throat, "I need a word with you."

"Come on, come with me, Malyshka."

"She can stay with your mother. I need to speak to you alone."

I kissed the side of Jules head and whispered. "I'll be right back."

I nodded at Alexei, telling him to stay with her.

I followed my father into his office and waited for it. He sighed and ran a hand over his face. "Is it true?"

"What's true?" I asked.

"That the beauty you have brought is Luciano's little sister."

I glared at my brother and nodded.

"I thought you put her with a family you could trust."

"Apparently not," I scoffed, "I'm dealing with it the best I can."

"Tell him where you found her." My brother added.

"You just don't know when…"

"So, where did you find her?"

"An auction," I mumbled.

"Come again, son. It sounded like you said she was at an auction."

"Because I did. I had to swoop in again and play the hero to keep her safe."

My father curled his lips.
My brother scoffed.
And me?
I knew I didn't play the hero.
I was the villain.

"But you didn't really save her, no?"

"I… did. I. Saved. Her."

"No. You. Didn't." Adrian growled. "You took her for yourself."

I took a few long strides and sized my brother up. I clenched my fists and grabbed him by the collar of his shirt. "You weren't there, Adrian. You didn't see how many predators were there. If I hadn't bought her, she would be dead. Once they found out whom she was, they would kill her and deliver her body to me."

"Vadim!" My father growled. "You need to keep your voice down."

I punched Adrian in the jaw and shoved him, causing him to stumble back. I closed my eyes and took a deep breath. When I opened my eyes, my father put his hands on my shoulders. "I have to ask."

"What?" I asked, but I already knew what he was going to say.

"Do you care for her?"

"Of course, I care. She's Luciano's sister."

"Here's another question and don't lie to me, son. Have you… have you touched her?"

Adrian snorted. "Of course, he has."

"Silence Adrian!" My father growled. "Leave us."

"But…" Adrian whined.

I threw him a smirk and nodded to the door. "Go on, I'm sure the women have a job for you to do."

Adrian rolled his eyes and shot back. "Oh yeah, maybe Jules needs some help."

"Leave now, before I throw you out. Your mother wants us to have a nice celebration today. And that's exactly what she's going to get. That means no fighting. No arguing. And under any circumstances, do not mention Luciano at the table. This girl has no idea he was her brother. To her, he was just a friend that protected her."

"Fine," Adrian mumbled under his breath as he stormed out of the room.

"I need you to listen to me, son." My father starts.

I knew where this was going.

"There's only one way to keep her protected." He said.

"I know," I breathed out.

"You have to make her your wife."

How would Alexei respond to this?

"You don't have to do it today, but soon, you need to make the preparations to wed Luciano's sister. After all, that was his last wish, yes?"

"He said to protect her," I growled. "Not get married to her."

"If you don't, I'll find someone who will. What about Alexei? He would make a good husband."

"Actually, that's not a bad idea."

My father widened his eyes and covered his mouth. "Oh. My. God. You've been with them both."

"And?" I raised a brow.

"Son, I'm not judging you. I think you would be the better husband."

"No. If they know she is to be my wife, it would be a target on her. Alexei is my best man and perfect for the job. Just in case this war goes south, Jules will be protected by Alexei and you will have a new King. You know, in case I don't make it."

"Don't say that, son. You'll take care of the problem and come out on top. All Kaslov Kings come out on top. It's in our blood."

The truth was, I wanted Jules and Alexei both by my side at all times. But I guess my father had other plans. The hard part would be getting Alexei to agree to it. I entered the kitchen and leaned in to whisper in Alexei's ear. "We need to talk."

Alexei froze.

"Relax, it's fine. I just need you to do something for me."

His body relaxed, but I knew better.
On the inside, he was freaking out.

Chapter 10

Jules

I could feel the tension between Vadim and Alexei throughout the dinner. Angelina prepared Solyanka, a thick soup that is plentiful enough to be a meal in itself. It was made with sausage, bacon, ham, and beef, as well as vegetables such as cabbage, carrots, onions, and potatoes. Chopped pickles and the traditional lemon slice garnish made the flavors burst in my mouth.

Vadim leaned over and whispered in my ear. "I can't wait to get you home."

He put his hand on my thigh and pulled my dress up over my knees. Everyone at the table was oblivious to what was happening. Everyone except for Vadim and Alexei. I glanced at Vadim and parted my thighs slightly. I turned my head and met Alexei's hungry gaze. He gripped my other thigh and pulled it over his leg.

"Now, for dessert." Angelina announced.

"Dessert sounds lovely, doesn't it, Malyshka?" Alexei whispered.

I nodded not being able to speak.

"Would you like to have some dessert, Jules?" Vadim's brother asked, a smirk forming on his lips.

"Yes, I would love some dessert."

He knew what Vadim and Alexei was up to. Vadim brushed his finger against my silk panties and murmured in my ear. "I would love some dessert too, baby girl."

I swallowed hard and tried to pull his hand away.

"Vadim…"

"Relax, baby girl. I just want to have a taste."

Angelina had two other women bring in a large cake on a tray with rollers. It said, Happy 50th Anniversary, Angelina and Boris!

"Thank you, everyone. I'm so happy to have all my sons together with us on this special day. For fifty years, I've been the one to put up with this man. And for fifty years, he loved and cherished me. Protected me from his enemies. I love you, Boris." Angelina kissed him and he kissed her back.

"I love you too, Angelina. Now, Vadim, it's time for you to do the same. I want you to find yours."

Vadim was getting married?

I jerked away from Vadim and Alexei as soon as I heard the words.

"Vadim, you will find a suitable wife and marry her. You will love her and cherish her as I have done with your mother."

I scooted my chair back and ran. I had no idea where, but I had to get away. Vadim lied to me. He made me fall for him, and I was stupid enough to think he felt the same. I pushed the door open and slammed the door. I locked it and fell to my knees. I could hear someone pounding on the door, but I ignored it.

"Malyshka, open the door." Vadim pleaded.

"Leave me alone. You lied to me! Used me!"

"Baby girl," Alexei whispered through the door, "Please, open the door."

"No," I sobbed.

I heard the doorknob rattle and click. I backed away from the door and prayed silently. The door busted open and Vadim was quick to scoop me in his arms. I averted my gaze, but he gripped my chin harshly and forced me to look at him. "I'm not getting married, Malyshka.

"What?"

"I'm not getting married… Alexei is… to you."

"W-what?" Alexei spluttered. "Boss…"

"You will be married to Alexei in a weeks' time, Jules."

"Vadim, I…" I started but he cut me off with a kiss.

"Baby girl, you will be married to Alexei on paper. It's for your protection. Nothing will change between us three. I will still continue to fuck you both as you will with me."

"Boss?" Alexei asked confused.

"Come here, Alexei."

Alexei stepped forward and bowed his head. Vadim leaned forward and kissed his lips. I couldn't help but get turned on being in the middle of these two men. When Vadim pulled away, he kissed me again and whispered against me. "Nothing will change, Malyshka."

"Take me home," I wanted them both. So. Damn. Bad.

"Let's go home, Alexei." Vadim ordered.

Vadim carried me out to the car and placed me in the backseat. However, Alexei joined us in the back too. I glanced at the driver seat and saw that Vadim's brother was in the driver seat. Vadim leaned forward and commanded him. "Take us home."

Vadim rolled the partition up and turned to me. "Straddle Alexei, I want to watch you fuck him."

"Right here… in the car?" I asked in a whisper.

"Yes, make love to your future husband."

Alexei pulled me over on his lap and circled my waist. "Yes, baby girl, make love to me."

Vadim pulled my dress up and ripped my panties off. I moaned when Vadim slipped two fingers inside me. He pumped me at a steady pace, while Alexei worked frantically to free his cock. I helped him reach inside to grip the base of his cock. Vadim retracted his fingers and Alexei replaced them with his cock. I arched my back and moaned as he thrust upward. He kissed me as I bounced up and down. Vadim pulled the top of my dress, freeing my breast. Alexei pulled away from my lips and pressed his face between them.

"Baby girl… god, you feel so good." He groaned.

Before I knew it, Vadim cupped my face and kissed me hard. This time, it was Alexei who was the more dominant one. Rougher. Demanding. Hard. Vadim kissed me gently as Alexei gripped my hips and slammed me back down on him. Harder with each time. Just as I was about to cum, the car stopped. And to my disappointment, Alexei pulled away. Vadim too.

"Don't worry, Malyshka, we're not done with you yet. Not by a long shot." Vadim murmured.

Alexei zipped his pants, but left his button open and his belt undone. Vadim, Alexei, and I entered the estate looking a total mess. While Vadim looked normal, Alexei and I looked like we went through a storm. My hair was messed up and my dress was a little ripped. Alexei's hair was disheveled and his shirt was untucked. They led me to Vadim's bedroom by the wrists. Vadim shoved me to the bed and began to undress.

"I'm on fire, Malyshka." Vadim growled.

"I need you… I need both of you." I whispered as I pulled down the top of my dress. Alexei took the bottom of my dress and ripped it off of me. I was completely naked for them. Needing them to touch me.

"Touch yourself, baby girl. Show us how wet our kitten is." Alexei demanded.

Alexei stripped off his clothes and stood at the side of the bed. He stroked his cock and took my pierced nipple between his thumb and index finger. I found myself moaning for more. Desperate. Wet. Vadim knelt between my thighs and forced my legs further apart.

"Is our kitten wet for us, Malyshka?" Vadim blew on me lightly. The coolness of his breath made me rock my hips.

"Yes, Daddy."

Vadim's eyes darkened as the words rolled off my tongue. I knew what calling him that did to him. It made his beast come alive. And I loved it. I loved everything about him. The way he called me Malyshka. Baby girl. How he handled me with care. But most of all, I loved it when he possessed my body and dominated me. That's the man I really craved.

"You want Daddy to come out to play with you, baby girl?"

I nodded and bit my lip.

"Well, that's unfortunate… because you're not getting one Daddy, you're getting two tonight." Vadim said, glancing at Alexei.

“Boss?”

“Tonight, you’re not Alexei, my second-in-command. Tonight, you will be Daddy Alexei. How does that sound?”

Alexei curved his lips and groaned as he stroked himself. “It sounds… good.”

“Do you think you can handle two dicks, Malyshka?”

“Yes,” I whispered.

“Stand up,” Vadim demanded, “Arms behind your back.”

Chapter 11

Vadim

Jules laid there frozen when I ordered her to stand. She sat up and stood at my command. I looked over to Alexei and nodded for him to help her. He released his cock to take her by the wrist. Alexei's eyes burned with lust as he positioned her to stand in front of me. He yanked her arms behind her back and whispered in her ear. "Stay just like this, baby girl."

"My sweet little, Malyshka." I said, "Do you really think you can handle us?"

"Yes," she whispered.

Alexei jerked her back against his chest and hissed. "Yes, what?"

I narrowed my eyes and gripped her chin hard. "You going to answer the question?"

"Yes," she repeated.

"Are you asking for a punishment?" I asked, my voice full of venom.

She shook her head.

"Baby girl, use your words."

I knew this was her way of punishing us to get back for what happened in the car. Our little kitten was on the verge of coming, but we stopped. Sure, we could've kept going. I decided I wanted her in my room instead.

I jerked her face and leaned in dangerously close to her. She gasped when I took her nipple between my finger and thumb, giving it a sharp pinch.

"Daddy, I'm sorry."

"Tell Alexei how sorry you are." I paused, "No, wait. I want you to turn around and face Alexei. Get on your knees and show him how sorry you are."

When she didn't attempt to turn around, Alexei spun her around and shoved her down. I held her wrist tightly and leaned down next to her ear. "Show him, Malyshka."

Jules struggled to break free, but I kept her in my dominant hold. Alexei stroked her cheek and hissed. "Open."

She opened her mouth and took him in her mouth. Alexei held her by the back of the neck and groaned. The soft sucking sounds made my cock twitch. I loved watching her with Alexei. It turned me on to know Alexei did too. I met Alexei's eyes and licked my lips. He reached around Jules and wrapped his hand around my length, stroking me softly. I covered his hand and helped him jerk faster and harder.

Alexei pulled out of Jules mouth and rasped. "I want to take her to the bed."

We untangled our bodies and Alexei laid back on the bed. He scooted back until his back hit the headboard. I helped Jules into bed and forced her to straddle Alexei. He spread his thighs and slid into her heat.

"How about we take this up a notch?" I suggested.

Alexei curved his lips and smirked as he thrust his hips. Jules moaned and rocked her hips as I placed each of her wrists on the back of the bed. "Keep your hands here. You move them and I'll make sure you receive a punishment."

Each time Alexei thrust into Jules; it was like she was being shocked. I could see her clench the back of the bed in attempt to hold on. Alexei's ass came off the mattress and I smiled. He was trying to make her let go. I had no idea how dominant Alexei was. I know now, I made the right choice when I allowed him to join us. He palmed her ass, his fingers digging into her skin. The harder he thrust; the more I could see Jules was about to fall.

"I-I can't, Daddy. I can't hold on anymore."

Jules cried out as she let go of the frame and fell back into my arms. But Alexei wasn't done yet. No. He kept thrusting into her like it would be the last time he was going to fuck her. Her body convulsed and that's when it happened, Alexei came hard. Filling her full of his seed. And I loved that we could make her feel this way. Her head fell back and she whimpered. "I'm sorry, Daddies."

"There, there, Malyshka. I'll make sure you don't' suffer… much."

Chapter 12

Jules

Vadim cuffed my right wrist while Alexei did the same to the left one. My nipples hardened against the cold wall.

Click.

Click.

"Vadim…"

"Silence!" Vadim hissed. "You've been a bad, bad girl, Malyshka."

My breath hitched as he stood behind me and leaned into my neck. His breath hit my ear as he whispered harshly. "Spread your thighs, Malyshka. You're going to receive a punishment for coming without permission."

I turned my head to see Alexei holding his belt. He folded it in half and took Vadim's place behind me.

"Alexei, p-please…"

I turned to my right to see Vadim watching Alexei and I. He nodded to Alexei to give him the order. I closed my eyes and clenched my fists. Vadim thought this was a punishment, but it really wasn't. It was something I craved. I came on purpose, knowing that he would punish me. Alexei knew it. I knew it. But Vadim, he had no idea he'd been set up. And when he figured it out, I feared of how bad the punishment would be. The real punishment.

Alexei brought the leather down on my back. Sharp pain shot through me. Excitement also ran through me too. I arched my back and faked a whimper.

Alexei murmured. "Good girl."

He brought the belt down again. This time on my lower back above my ass. I cried out. The leather burned but in a good way. I loved the pain.

"Harder, Alexei. Show our little kitten what happens to disobedient girls. I want her ass glowing."

Alexei did as Vadim commanded him.

I met Vadim's dark eyes.

He narrowed them and stood.

"Stop!" Vadim demanded, "I have a better idea. Release Jules and chain her to the bed."

"Vadim, please…"

Vadim stormed across the room and stood behind me. He gripped my hips and hissed in my ear. "You think you pulled one past me, Malyshka? You want to be punished and I intend to do just that. In fact, I have the perfect punishment in mind."

Vadim pulled away from me and wrapped his arm around Alexei's waist. "Chain her to the bed. Our little Jules is going to get one hell of a punishment."

"Boss?" Alexei met my bewildered expression and shook his head. Vadim knew. But didn't know Alexei knew too.

I glanced behind me as Vadim feathered his lips over Alexei's mouth and pushed him against the wall. Vadim shifted his gaze meeting my panicked expression and curved his lips. "Is this what you want, Malylshka?"

Vadim crushed his lips against Alexei's mouth. My mouth went dry at the sight. Vadim kissed him fierce for a few moments and pulled away. "Do you really want me to punish you as I see fit?"

"Yes," I breathed out, "Punish me, I deserve it."

Suddenly, I was unchained by Alexei and Vadim. I dropped my head as Alexei led me back to the bed. Alexei pushed me to the bed and began to restrain me. I raised my head to see Vadim leaning on the post with his arms above his head. "Remember, you asked for this."

Alexei tugged on the chains and nodded. "She's secure, boss."

Vadim smirked, "Ankles too. And Alexei, insert the egg vibrator. If she wants to cum, she will damn sure cum. Over and over… until her body gives out."

I begged Alexei silently.

"I'm sorry baby girl, but it's orders from the boss." Alexei said as he wrapped the cuffed around my ankles and buckled them tight.

Vadim watched as Alexei inserted the vibrator inside me. I jerked when it came to life and arched my back. All I could feel is pleasure. The toy buzzed, making me thrash against the cuffs. Vadim walked back across the room, lounging back on the sofa. He put his arms over the back of it and watched in amusement as I fought the urge to cum.

"Come here, Alexei. Daddy time is over for you."

"W-what?" Alexei spluttered.

"This is a double punishment. You didn't think you could slip one past me, did you?"

"N-no, boss," Alexei whispered in defeat.

"Come here and kneel for me. I want Jules to see just how desperate my second-in-command is for his boss."

"Fu…uck!" I moaned loudly as I felt myself coming.

Vadim's eyes never leave mine as he forces Alexei's mouth down on his engorged member. My thighs tremor as another wave of pleasure comes over me. Sweat covers my body, making me glisten under the light. Like a jewel. Vadim groans as Alexei continues to suck greedily.

"Vadim, please." I whimpered.

My body is a quivering mess. Vadim lifts his head and pulls Alexei's mouth off of him. He cupped the side of his face and murmured. "Do you think she's learned her lesson?"

"Yes," he whispered. "She has."

"Hmm," Vadim throws me a smirk. "I don't know. Jules was a very bad girl."

"I-I'll accept her punishment, boss. Whatever you decide, I'll take it."

"Anything I want, hmm? Even if I make you watch Jules fuck me?"

"Yes, boss."

"Very well, go take the toy out and bring her to me."

Alexei released me from the restraints and took the toy out, turning it off. He gently picked me up. I wrapped my arms around his neck as he carried me to Vadim. He placed me on his lap with my legs on each side of him.

"I'm sorry, Sir." I whispered as tears ran down my rosy cheeks.

"I know, but rules are rules. Are you going to be a good girl for me?"

"Yes, Sir, I understand."

Vadim wiped my tears and murmured. "Good girl."

Vadim lifted my ass and slid inside. He crushed his lips against mine, thrusting his tongue inside my mouth. I melted under his touch. Another pair of hands palmed my ass as Vadim continued to fill me to the hilt.

"Fuck, Malyshka." Vadim groaned. "Fuck her, Alexei. You have my permission."

"Baby girl, I'm going to fuck your ass now." Alexei's deep voice said.

I whimpered when he positioned the head of his cock at the entrance. I arched my back and moaned when he pushed into me.

"Please…" I moaned against Vadim's mouth.

"Relax, baby girl." Alexei whispered. "I'll be gentle."

Inch by inch, Alexei eased deeper inside and cupped my breasts. Desire rippled through me being ravaged by two men. They were beasts as they took me. Vadim claimed me. And Alexei? He marked my skin with his teeth as he took my ass. I might be owned by Vadim, but they both owned my heart. Mind, body, and soul. I was theirs.

To possess.

To mark as theirs.

To fuck.

And if I was a bad girl, I was theirs to punish.

To break.

And after I take my punishment, they'll put me back together.

Piece by piece.

"Baby girl… fuck." Alexei grunted in my ear as he spilled into me.

"Malyshka, I'm coming. Cum for me. Cum. Malyshka."

My stomach tightens at his command. My walls close in and cry out as he fills me up.

"In a week, you will be married to Alexei. Tomorrow, you will be fitted for your wedding dress. Regina will take your measurements and have the dress sized to fit you."

I bit my lip.

"What's wrong?"

"I… want to marry both of you."

"You will, but not yet. Not until I make sure it's safe for you."

I laid my head on his chest and sighed. Alexei and Vadim pulled out of me as I closed my eyes. Sleep takes over me, but that's when my nightmares come. Not really dreams. Just memories of my past.

The next morning, I wake up fully clothed. Regina gently shakes me to let me know it's time.

"I'm sorry about before." I blurted out.

"Sorry for what?" Regina asks.

"For trying to hurt you. I was scared."

She chuckles softly. "All is forgotten."

I blow out a sigh of relief.

She starts to take my measurements. When she's done, she writes down everything on her clipboard.

"He loves you. Of course, he would never admit it out loud, but he does. He already broke his number one rule by bringing you here."

"What rule?"

"The boss never goes to auctions. He's never bought a human, until you. You're special."

Special?

I wasn't' special. Just lucky he saved me. Again.

Chapter 13

Vadim

In a week, Jules and Alexei would be married. Was I jealous? No. Why? Because I loved them both. After the threat was eliminated, I would be married to them. I drank my whiskey and sighed as I looked out my window. Rain poured down and thunder struck. I turned as I heard a knock at the door. I answered it, revealing Regina and Jules.

"Thank you, Regina. Tell Alexei to meet me in the basement in twenty minutes."

"Of course," she bowed in respect and nudged Jules inside my room.

I closed the door and pinned Jules to it. I kissed her, causing her to let out a moan. Only I could make her melt under my touch. I squeezed her right breast and ground my hips against her. I bet if I checked, she would be ready for me. Wet and horny. I pulled away from her lips and wrapped one hand around her throat.

"Are you wet, Malyshka?" I asked.

"Mmmhmm, Sir." She moaned.

I reached under her dress and cupped her sex. I squeezed hard and growled. "Who does this belong to, kitten?"

"You," she whimpered. "I belong to you."

"Me what, Malyshka?"

"I belong to you, Sir."

"Daddy." I corrected her. "From now on you will call me Daddy."

"Daddy, please."

"What do you want, little one?"

"You… I want you, Daddy."

"Tell me what you wan me to do to you."

"Use me, Daddy. My body is yours to do as you please."

I pulled away from her, but only to strip off her dress. I smiled down at her when her nipples hardened. Her piercings had healed. That was good. Because that means she's ready to be taken to the next level.

I took each nipple between my index finger and thumb, giving them a pinch. Jules arched her back and cried out.

"Arms behind your back, kitten. Thighs spread."

Jules did as I said and whimpered. I know I told Alexei to meet me in the basement in twenty minutes, but right now, I was craving Jules. I released her nipples and ran my hands down her chest to her hips. I jerked her forward and ground my hips against her. My dick pressed against her belly through my pants. I could see her fight the urge to touch me.

I crushed my lips against her mouth and groaned. She tasted sweet. But I knew better to think she was innocent. She was a filthy little slut. And right now, she was begging me with her body. I pulled away, leaving her breathless.

"I'm going to ask you again, Malyshka. What you want me to do with you?"

"Fuck me," she whispered. "I want you to bend me over and have your way with me."

"Get on the bed and kneel up for me. If you want me to fuck you, I'll fuck you real good."

Jules bent over the edge of the bed and raised her ass, thighs spread out for me. I walked to the bed and trailed one finger down her spine. She shivered, rocking her hips.

"Beautiful." I murmured. "So fucking beautiful and all mine."

I unzipped my pants, pulling my erect member through the slit and wrapped my hand around my cock. I teased her with the head and leaned over her. I kissed her neck and thrust into her without warning. She cried out in pleasure and threw her head back. Too bad Alexei wasn't here. I would love to see him fuck her pretty mouth.

"Harder, Daddy!" she cried.

"There she is, Daddy's filthy little girl. My dirty little slut." I groaned, thrusting my hips.

Fuck me!

She may not be a virgin anymore, but she's still just as tight as one.

"Cum for me, Malyshka. Milk my dick." I demanded.

Jules' body quivered and squeezed me tight. I felt her pussy contract and cum hard.

"Gonna cum now, Malyshka. I'm going to put a baby inside you."

I came hard. Probably the hardest I'd ever done in my life. I kissed her neck and whispered in her ear. "I love you, Malyshka."

Jules collapsed, her breaths still ragged. But still, she breathed out to me. "I love you too, Daddy."

I left Jules to catch her breath to meet Alexei in the basement. When I entered it, he was too busy torturing the woman. Not that I blame him. She promised to keep Jules safe and lied to me. To us. She hurt Jules. Sold her to Yuri. And in return, he put her in the auction. Now, it's time for her to meet her fate. Pay for ever betraying my trust.

I folded my arms over my chest and gave the woman a sardonic grin. She cried out in pain when he plunged a knife into her thigh.

"Alexei, it's time." I told him. "Kill the bitch."

Alexei turned to glance at me and smirked. "With pleasure, boss."

"S-spare me, please!" she cried out.

"Any last words, cunt?" Alexei asked.

She shook her head as tears rolled down her face. Alexei pulled out the knife and held it to her throat. In one swipe, he slit her throat. Blood poured out as her body went limp. Alexei placed the knife down on the metal tray and took off his gloves. He turned to me and nodded.

"Come here," I demanded. "Give me a kiss."

Alexei walked to me and wrapped his arms around my neck. He brushed his lips against mine and kissed me. I deepened the kiss and pulled him flush to my body. I pulled away and murmured. "Five days, Alexei. In five days, you will be married to Jules. Are you ready to become a husband?"

"Yes, boss. I am ready."

"Good. Tonight, we celebrate your engagement. And tomorrow, you will pick out a suit of your choice."

"Boss?"

"Yes."

"I… I love you."

"And I love you too, Alexei. I love you and Jules so much."

"I love you and Jules so much, too."

"Come. Jules is waiting for us in the bedroom. I believe we have an engagement to celebrate."

I led Alexei to the bedroom and smiled at Jules. She was dressed in a bathing suit. Red. Skimpy. It made my dick spring to life.

"Change of plans. Let's go to the pool."

"Boss?"

"Strip down to your boxers, Alexei. We're going swimming. And you Jules, come give Daddy a kiss. Both of us."

Jules stood up from the bed and stepped forwards. I closed the space and captured her lips. Wrapping my arms around her waist, I pressed her against my hardness. She moaned, giving me the perfect opportunity to deepen the kiss. I pulled away and pushed her toward Alexei.

"Now, give him a kiss. Kiss him like you just kissed me."

I stood behind her and ran my hands down her back and back up, reaching around her waist. I cupped each breast and squeezed, pushing them together. Nothing was hotter than seeing my most trusted man kiss Jules. The more I thought about it, the harder I got. Alexei devoured her mouth and groaned as she ran her hands down his chest, making her way to the waistband of his boxer briefs.

I lowered my hands and held Jules by the waist. Sure, I could take her from behind and fuck her ass while Alexei filled her pussy, but that would be too easy. Besides, this is a celebration. I would take them both down to the pool and drink some whiskey while I watched Alexei and Jules get wet. Clothes optional. Hopefully, they stripped off their damn clothes and give me a show. I led them both down to the pool and poured Alexei and I a whiskey. I poured Jules a glass of red wine. Her favorite. We all picked up our glass and raised them up. I grinned at Alexei.

"To Jules and Alexei, the happy couple. That's what the public will think. But what they won't know is it's just a ploy to lure out the dirty bastard. When the time comes, I will join you and Jules in holy matrimony. Be joined with you. But first, we take out the trash. Starting with that bastard foster dad, Jules."

We took a sip and fuck me, if I didn't want to join Alexei and Jules. But tonight, it wasn't about me. It was about Alexei and Jules. To be truthful, it was more about giving Jules the best night of her life. They entered the pool and kissed. Alexei pushed her against the edge of the pool and reached in the water. I took a seat and sipped my whiskey.

"You won't be needing these, baby girl." Alexei growled, throwing her bottoms on the deck.

Alexei ripped her top and threw it next to her bottoms. Next, he took his boxer briefs off and turned her around. Her nipple rings glittered under the sun. he pushed her over the edge of the pool and grunted when he entered her. I loved watching them. It turned me on to see them both together. Mostly… I enjoyed watching Jules come apart for Alexei.

I would avenge Jules. Rip each and every motherfucker apart for hurting her. Make them wish they were dead. I would kill them… slowly. Be the monster I was believed to be.

"Harder, Alexei!" Jules cried out as he took her from behind.

Fuck me!
Time to join in on the fun.

And after… I would take Alexei just like he's doing with Jules.
But first, I would fill Jules mouth with my dick and fuck her pretty mouth.

She says she wants me to break her.
I will.
Piece by piece.
But not before I kill Yuri for harming my property.

Let the games begin, Yuri.
Only the strong will survive.

And it damn sure isn't going to be you.

Jules thinks I'm an Angel.
Nope, not an Angel.
I'm the worst kind of monster.
The Devil reincarnated.
A Dirty Don.

"Open up, Malyshka. It's time to feed my beast." I told her, dropping my shorts.

Chapter 14

Yuri

"Have you brought me news?" I asked the man.

"I have, Mr. Volkov."

"And?" I questioned.

"Everything is going as planned. Vadim bought the bait. Alexei is to be married to Jules."

I clapped and smiled. "Good. When is the wedding?"

"In three days, Mr. Volkov. Shall I send…"

"No!" I snapped. "Just remember the plan. Take Alexei, but don't harm Jules. Leave that one for me to hurt. I want to see Alexei's face when he realizes who the traitor really is. Who would have thought it would be Vadim's own damn brother that stabbed him in the back. And when we capture them, I want you to send Vadim an email. Make sure he knows that we mean business."

"You mean…"

"Yes, Adrian, you are going to fuck the little bitch in front of Alexei and record it. For now, we wait for the pieces on the chess board to fall in place. The day of the wedding, you take the team and drag Alexei to the warehouse by any means necessary. I'll have a few of my girls sneak in as hairdressers and drug her. It will be a piece of cake."

"Of course, Mr. Volkov."

"Call me Yuri."

"They share her." He whispered. "Vadim and Alexei have fallen in love with the girl."

"Good. That makes everything so much better. I'll enjoy ripping Vadim and Alexei's heart out when I break their precious Angel in a million pieces. Then, we'll see who the bigger man is."

"What do you get out of it?" he asked.

"I'll take the liberty of ruining Vadim and taking over his throne."

"But…"

"Hush, no more talking, Adrian." I murmured and crushed my lips against his mouth.

Within a few days, Vadim's world would come crashing down. Let it be a lesson to those who cross me. It's my revenge for killing my Corina. He opened fire in my club and killed my wife. Now, it's time to give him a little payback.

I pulled away from Adrian's mouth and cupped his balls. "So full. Do you need to release some tension?"

"Yes, please."

I patted his cheek softly and whispered. "Would you like to borrow one of my girls or would you rather get fucked up the ass?"

"Fuck me, Yuri. Fuck my tight asshole."

Chapter 15

Jules

I had a bad feeling. Something didn't feel right. The wedding preparations had been made. My dress had been sized to fit me perfectly. And Alexei's suit had been picked out. In two days, I would be married to him. Alexei assured me everything was fine. I knew it wasn't. Not when Yuri was still out there.

I remember Yuri's last words at the auction.

"Now it begins, my sweet Jules. Let's hope you make it out alive. Well, that's if Vadim doesn't kill you before the game ends."

I glanced to my left and saw Alexei sleeping soundly. To my right, Vadim was already awake. How could I tell him what Yuri was planning without him getting mad at me? The last thing I wanted was to upset him. Not after all he's done for me. He saved me. Clothed me. Cared for me. And Alexei, what would he say?

"Jules," Vadim smiled. "I can hear the wheels turning in your head. What troubles you, Malyshka?"

"I… I remembered something the night of the auction."

Vadim scooped me in his arms and narrowed his eyes. "Tell me."

"You'll be so mad at me." I whispered.

"No, I won't be angry with you. I won't hurt you unless you ask me to." He promised.

"Yuri… he said something to me that night. Something I fear for your life. I don't want… I don't want to lose you or Alexei."

"You won't, my love. Now, tell me what he said."

I took a deep breath and whispered. "It's all a game, Vadim. He wants to ruin you. He told me, "Now it begins, my sweet Jules. Let's hope you make it out alive. Well, that's if Vadim doesn't kill you before the game ends."

Vadim cursed under his breath and kissed the top of my head. "I swear to you, I won't let anything happen to you. In a few days, you'll be married to Alexei and I'll avenge you. Every last person that hurt you will die at my hands."

"I'm scared for you… for Alexei. What if…"

Vadim placed his finger against my lips and murmured. "No, I don't want you to think like that. I'll protect you until my last dying breath. Alexei too. We love you too much to let anything happen to you."

"Promise?"

"I promise, Malyshka. You will always be protected."

He pulled me onto his lap and kissed my lips softly. It wasn't like before. This kiss was gentle. Full of promise. Emotions. Something I'd yet to see with him. He held my face and deepened the kiss.

"Make love to me, Vadim." I whispered against his lips.

"No, not yet. I haven't had my breakfast yet."

"And neither have I." I heard Alexei say.

Vadim pushed me on my back and spread my thighs. He pulled me to him and ran his tongue upward on my inner thigh. My body was on fire for both men. Alexei stroked Vadim, causing a desire to make me a wanton whore. Vadim sucked and licked my clit, flicking his tongue against the metal barbell. Just as I was about to cum, Vadim pulled away.

"Alexei, Jules, get down there and get my dick nice and wet."

Alexei and I knelt between his legs and peered up to him. Alexei wrapped his hand around his shaft and ran his tongue around the head. Vadim threw his head back and groaned as I kissed the opposite side.

"Fuck, so good." Vadim said. "So damn good."

Alexei and I met halfway and crushed our lips against each other. Our tongues clashed as we sucked the head. I felt a hand clamp down on the back of my neck. At first I thought it was Vadim. But no, it was Alexei shoving Vadim's dick in my mouth. I widened my eyes as Alexei forced more inside. Inch by inch. Vadim may own me, but both men had forced their way into my heart.

"Such a good girl for us." Alexei praised. "Now, relax your throat while I take you from behind."
Both men made love to me. One in my pussy. The other, he made love to my mouth. And after, Alexei filled me with his seed. One way or another, I was bound to get pregnant. The only question that lingered… whose baby would I be carrying? Vadim's or Alexei's?

I just hope for all of our sake, the wedding goes as planned.

Tomorrow, Vadim will make the engagement public.
And after… the wedding.

Chapter 16

Vadim

"Are you sure about this, son?" My father asked me.

"Yes, it's the only way to keep her safe. Luciano… I promised him…"

"You need to tell her the truth about Luciano. She deserves to know he was more than just a friend."

I sighed. "I know, but not yet. Not until the threat has been illuminated. Then after, I'll tell her the truth."

I knew he was right. Luciano was Jules' brother. She should know who he really was.

"The press is waiting for you."

My father followed me out to the podium. Flashes of light blinded me. I clipped the microphone to my tie and cleared my throat. "Thank you for coming today."

Flash. Flash. Flash.
Click. Click. Click.

"Is it true?" One person asked.

I held my hand up. "Wait for questions in a minute. Alexei, my best friend, has found his true love. In a few days, he's getting married to Jules. They are happy, therefore, I am happy for him. A royal wedding will take place in the Koslov Vineyard."

"Is it true that Jules is Luciano Patrick's sister."

"Rumors. She is a common American girl who fell madly in love with Alexei."

The lie fell from my lips like it was nothing. They didn't need to know who she really was. This wasn't for the press. It was more for Yuri Volkov. To let him know I was on to his game.

"One last thing before I go. Yuri Volkov, if you're listening and I know you are, I do hope you can attend the wedding. I know you've been wanting to meet the girl Alexei has fallen for. I extend my invitation to you and whoever else thinks they can beat me at my own game."

I took off the microphone and set it down on the podium. I was about to leave with my father when a familiar voice made me freeze in my tracks. "I do hope you can play by my rules this time."

I turned and clenched my jaw. Bastard. Yuri smiled, knowing I couldn't do anything. Not with so many innocent people around. That would make his fucking day. I mirrored his grin and said. "I look forward to seeing you there."

"It's a date then, eh? I'm sure you'll love the surprise I have planned for you."

"Come on, let's go." My father hissed. "He'll get his, but now isn't the time. Too many prying eyes."

I turned and walked off the stage with my father. He was worried for me. I could tell by the urgency of his voice. When we made it back to the car, he sighed. "I'll ask you one more time, son. Are you sure this is a good idea?"

"Is it a good idea? No. But it's what needs to be done. I'll triple the security if I have to, but I need to see this plan through. It's the only way to put an end to his insanity."

"And what if it backfires? What if it costs you everything you've ever worked for?"

"As long as Jules is safe, I don't care. If I die in the process, she'll have Alexei to take good care of her."

"No… we'll find another way to take him down."

"The wedding has already been planned and preparations have already been done. There's no going back until everyone responsible for hurting her is dead and gone. He needs to pay for what he did to Luciano… to our family."

"And he will." My father lets out a harsh breath. "Adrian has gone off the grid."

I whipped my head to the side. "What?!"

"He's been acting strange lately. He's been getting anonymous phone calls and meeting with someone in private."

"You think he's a rat?"

"I don't know, but something fishy is going on. He's very secretive… very discreet."

"But why?"
"I don't know and that's why I've doubled security with your mother."

Could my brother be a rat?
Changed sides with us?

"I can…"

"No, I got it under control. You've got a lot on your plate right now. The most important thing is to keep Jules safe. And Vadim… keep your friends close but your enemies closer. You feel like something isn't right, you get Alexei, Jules, and yourself out."

His driver dropped me off at my estate. I stepped into my home and narrowed my eyes when I saw Adrian had made himself at home. Before, it would be fine. But now… I'm not sure if I want him here.

"Vadim, so nice to see you." Adrian grinned.

"Adrian, you should have called. Where's Alexei?"

"He's with your little Jules tending to her."

"What the hell are you talking about?!"

"She's not feeling so good. Been running a fever for the past hour. Hence, why I'm here."

"Well, I'm here now. You can leave."

"I believe congrats is in order."

"Thank you, but if you don't mind, I'd like you to leave. Now."

I watched as he left the estate and called one of my men to follow him. If he's been up to no good, I'd find out. But first, I needed to find out what happened to Jules. I entered Alexei's room and met Alexei's panicked expression. I shifted my gaze to Jules and narrowed my eyes. I knew what this was. It was no flu. Or a virus. Our little Angel had been drugged. I could tell by the look in her eyes.

"How?"

"I don't know. She had lunch and she was fine. Then, Adrian…"

"Adrian!" I growled. "Fuck, how bad is she? What did he give her?"

"He brought her a box of chocolates. Why?"

"My father thinks he's switched sides."

"Motherfucker! And I just… it's all my fault."

"No, don't blame yourself. You couldn't have known. I just found out myself."

"Vadim," Jules groaned. "Vadim."

"She's been doing that for the past ten minutes. I drew her blood to find out what he gave her. Saveli should be back soon with the results."

I shrugged off my jacket and threw it on the floor. Inching closer, I watched as Jules clenched the sheets in her fists. I sat next to her and cupped her cheek. "Shh Malyshka, I'm here. We're both here with you."

"Vadim, help me." She whimpered.

"Shh, just rest. It will pass soon." I promised her.

I glanced at Alexei and gave him a reassuring smile. I grabbed his hand and squeezed hard. My way of telling him it would all be okay. But… would it? Hell if I know.

"She was asking question about him." Alexei whispered. "I think she knows."

I sighed when I heard a knock at the door. I nodded to Alexei to answer it. It was probably Saveli with the results. But to my surprise, it wasn't. Arianna bowed her head as she held an envelope in her hand. Alexei took it from her and ripped it open. And by the news, I'm guessing it's not good. Alexei took deep breaths as he read the results.

"It's the same damn drug, boss. The same one…" he whispered.

He didn't have to finish his sentence. I knew. And so did Arianna. I could hear Arianna give me an apology before Alexei slammed his fist into the wall. "Go back to Saveli, Arianna. Tell him I said thank you."

She nodded and scurried away.

I left Jules side to take the paper from Alexei. Now I know why he's so pissed. At the bottom was a result for a pregnancy test.

Positive.
Jules is carrying a child.

"Hey, look at me." I demanded Alexei. "It's going to be okay. She's going to be just fine."

"How can you know that? What if… what if that drug makes her lose the baby?"

"Then, we'll get revenge for that. Change of plans, I'll have the priest come tonight. No ceremony. Just rings and paperwork that says you're married to her."

"The wedding… what about that?"

"Let me worry about that and you worry about your fiancée. If I have to, I'll have Arianna step in as your Jules. The wedding will go on as planned."

"Boss, I don't know." Alexei trailed off. "I think we should call it off and take Jules away from this."

"That's not a bad idea. I'll arrange for Saveli and Arianna to get you out of the country."

"Not without you, boss."

"You will do as I say and that's a direct order. Do you understand?"

"Yes, boss."

"Good, now let's enjoy the next few days with Jules. After this is all over, we'll reunite and become one. I promise you."

                              Chapter 17

Jules

My head pounded as I tried to sit up. There was an ache between my thighs. A
burning desire to be touched. Almost… like when… after the auction. The time
Vadim bought me and brought me home. Vadim gently pushed me back down.
Next to me, Alexei brought a glass to my lips and forced me to drink. My throat
burned. Everything burned.

"Take it easy, Malyshka." Vadim murmured.

"W-what happened to me?" I asked.

"The bastard drugged you."

I blinked, trying to remember what happened. Nothing. Not even a flash of a
memory. I remember Alexei feeding me. Then, Vadim's brother showing up.
Then… nothing.

"Who?" I pushed for more information.

"Adrian, my brother. He… drugged you."

I could see Alexei and Vadim exchanging glances with each other. There was
something they weren't telling me. Something important. Something happened
while I was out. Bad. I knew it was too good to be true. Nothing ever went my
way. Just as soon as I was happy, it was snatched away from me. Ripped away.
And I had a feeling it had to do with my foster dad and Yuri.

"Vadim," I whispered. "Tell me."

"Malyshka, you're pregnant. The wedding is off and I'm sending you and Alexei
out of the country. I'll deal with this and when it's over, we'll be reunited as one.
But for now, I have a priest coming to marry you and Alexei."

"No, please. Don't send me away."

"Just for a little while. Alexei can keep you safe."

"I don't want to lose you." I wrapped my arms around his neck and cried into his chest.

"Don't cry, Malyshka. It's not good for the baby." Vadim said as he ran his hand up and down my back.

Alexei set the glass down and pulled my legs on his lap. He massaged my feet, making heat pool between my legs. Drugs. It's got to be the drugs.

The baby!
Oh my…

I'm pregnant. But who's the father?
Vadim… or Alexei?

"I'm pregnant." I whispered. "The baby, is it okay?"

"Shh, it will be fine. Everything will be fine, Malyshka." Alexei assured me.

"The priest will be here shortly." Vadim said, placing a kiss to my lips.

Married.
I was going to be married to Alexei.

"But first, we want to do things right. If you can't have a traditional wedding, at least let Alexei propose to you."

Alexei stood up from the bed and sunk to his knee. He took my hand and kissed my knuckles. "Baby girl, Jules, we love you. I knew once Vadim bought you that you would be his Queen. My baby girl. Ours. I don't know what happened, but I fell for your baby blues. The way you captivated our hearts. The warmth in your voice. I knew… we couldn't let you go. Will you marry me? And when the time comes, will you marry us both."

I nodded. "Yes, I love you both so much. Vadim might have bought me… saved me, but you both own my heart. I would love to be yours both. But for now, I'll marry you, Alexei."

Alexei slid the ring on my finger. I could hardly believe it. If only Vadim had never pushed me away when I was sixteen, would I already be married to him? Would he ever shared me with Alexei. I know it's not your average Cinderella story, but in my world, it was. Everything was perfect. My two dark Princes.

"After you are married to Alexei, you will make love to your husband. And I'll sit back and watch you consummate your marriage."

"You're not joining?" I asked.

"Not this time. This time, I'll enjoy watching Alexei pleasure you. Ravish you. Make you cum until you can't feel your legs."

Knock. Knock.

Vadim answered the door, letting the priest inside and closed the door.

"Mr. Koslov, it's always a pleasure doing business with you."

"Thanks for coming on short notice. You weren't followed, were you?"

"No. I did as you asked. My twin brother is dressed like me and I snuck out through the tunnels. Shall we begin?"

Alexei took my hand and led me to the priest.

"So glad to finally meet the woman who has melted Vadim and Alexei's heart."

The priest thrust a large manila envelope to Vadim and cleared his throat. "Do you have the rings?"

Alexei reached into his pocket and pulled out two gold bands. He slipped one in my hand and kissed my temple. "Are you ready, baby girl?"

"Yes, I'm ready."

"Alexei, Jules, join hands and repeat after me. This ring represents my love for you. I promise to love, cherish and be loyal to you. With this ring, I thee wed. Forever, until my last breath."

Alexei and I repeated his words.

"I now pronounce you husband and wife. Alexei, you may kiss your bride."

Alexei cupped my cheeks and kissed me. Our lips molded perfectly. It was like I was in a fairytale. A demented one, but still, my happy ever after. Only, I wasn't sure it would be. Alexei and I would have to leave the country. And Vadim? He was going to take his revenge on Yuri. My foster dad. And anyone else that got in the way. Blood would be shed. Lives would be lost. I just hope it wasn't Vadim or Alexei that fell victim to that. Or… me.

"Thank you for your service, Carlos."

Vadim opened the envelope and placed the paper on the table, handing Alexei a pen. Alexei took it and signed his name on the line. He then, handed it to me and whispered. "Sign your name, baby girl."

I scribbled my name and blew out a harsh breath. "So, that's it?"

"That's it, baby girl. For now, you're my wife. But after it's safe, you'll be our wife to do with as we please."

I smiled. "I like the sound of that."

"Good, you'll love it, I promise you." Alexei promised.

Vadim paid the priest and showed him out. When he returned, he took a seat on his sofa. He relaxed and licked his lips as Alexei pulled my dress over my head.

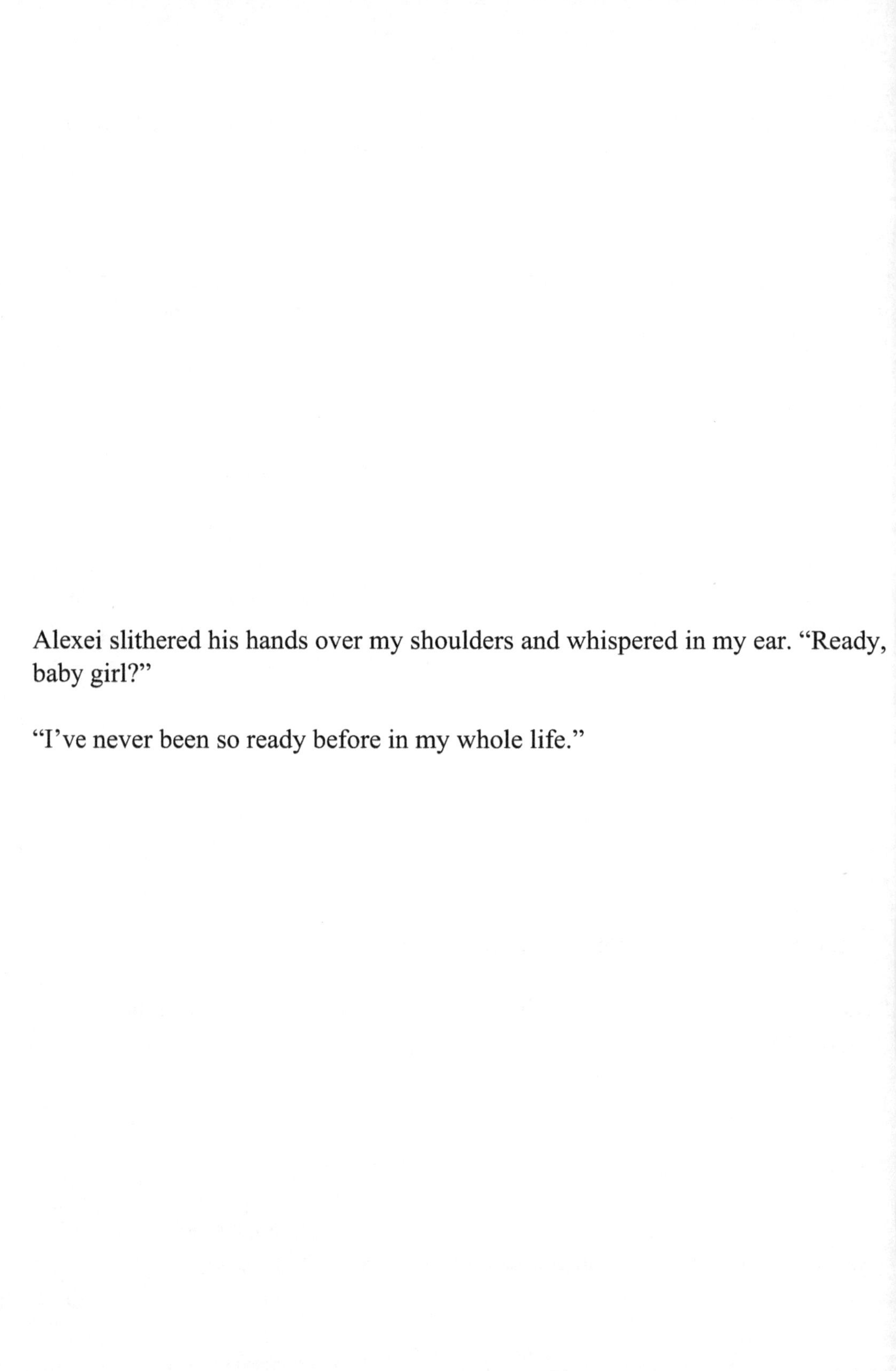

Alexei slithered his hands over my shoulders and whispered in my ear. "Ready, baby girl?"

"I've never been so ready before in my whole life."

Epilogue

Alexei

Two weeks later

Snap. Crackle. Pop.

Smoke billowed in the air as glass and debris crunched under my boots. Fire blazed in the distance.

How the fuck did this happen?

I always heard before you die, you see the light. Not me. Not even when I was knocked out. And not when I heard the blast. But Jules, where was she? The only thing I see is smoke and fire. I can hear the screams. Women begging to be spared. I glanced at their faces.

Thank fuck!
None of them are her.
Where are you, baby girl?

I staggered through the wreckage, holding my side. Desperately searching for her. Each time I hear another frantic voice, I silently pray.

Please, don't be her.
Don't let anything happen to her or the baby.

Because if it does, a war will break out.

So far, I haven't been spotted by the men who blew up the entire block. It's only a matter of time until they figure out who I really am. That's why I need to find Jules and get the fuck out. Quickly.

My blood runs cold when I hear it. Her weak voice calling out to me.

"Alexei, please… help me."

It's faint, but there's no denying it her. My wife. My delicate Jules.

I swallow hard as I cast my head downward. She reaches out to grab my ankle. The sight of my baby girl is enough to bring me to my knees. I crouch down, throwing the debris off her ankles.

"Alexei," Jules cries out. "It hurts."

"Shh, baby girl, Can you walk?"

I hear Jules start to cry again when I inspect her injured ankle. But nothing could prepare me for what I see next. I shift my gaze to her belly. And fuck me, it nearly kills me. Fresh blood stains the front of her dress right between her thighs.

"No, goddammit, no!"

I cradle her to my chest and kiss her lips. "I'm going to get you out of here, baby girl."

"It hurts." She cries softly.

"Shh, don't talk. Save your strength."

I pick her up and stand up to sneak away. I back up and freeze when I feel the cold metal of a knife to the back of my neck.

"Don't fucking move! The boss has been looking all over for you. The both of you."

I have no choice but to do as I'm told. I'm unarmed. Injured. I lost my phone. I'm royally screwed. I squeezed my eyes shut and took a deep breath.

"Turn around." Another voice says with a thick Russian accent.

I turn around slowly, hoping and praying it's not who I think it is. And it is.

"Hello, friend. I've been looking everywhere for you. Thank you for delivering the little slut to her rightful owner."

"You won't…"

"Get away with this? I already have. Grab the girl and Vadim's little boyfriend."

I tried to fight them, but it was useless. They had me at an advantage. I'm hurt. So is Jules. The only thing I can do is admit defeat. I just hope they don't harm Jules anymore than they have. I need her. Vadim needs her. The last thing I see is his sadistic grin as I fall into darkness.

(Coming late 2020-early 2021! Vadim, Jules, and Alexei's story continues.)
Owned By The Boss

Vadim

Fate brought her back to me. I didn't save her out of the goodness of my heart. I.
Wanted. Her. To own her. Possess her. So I bought her. Shared her with my
second-in-command. I realized then I didn't just want her. I wanted both of them.

In reality, I didn't save her.
She saved me.
I wanted forever with her.
With him.

And then...
Poof!
Gone.
Just like that.
My life turned upside down.

I was a fool.
Betrayed.
By my own blood.

I'll search to the end of the Earth until I find them. Wage war on anyone who gets
in my way.

Betray me?
I'll kill you.
Stand in my way?
I'll pulverize you.
And if you try to stop me?
You're as good as dead.

Through the blood, smoke, and fire, I'll get my revenge. Kill everyone responsible.
Even if I have to sacrifice my life to bring them home.

Prologue

Vadim

In the darkness, there's a tunnel. At the end is light. But me, I'm not going down there. The only way for me is to embrace the darkness. Douse the light with my evil soul. So much has happened. And for what? For my life to fall apart? To not know if I could have done something to save them is torture. Absolute fucking torture.

"Boss, you're going to fall and hurt yourself." Alexei's replacement warned.

I clenched the bottle in my hand and took another drink. Nothing could numb the pain of losing the two people I loved the most. Hell, I even tried to kill myself. I tried, but Regina came and talked me down.

"Shall I go fetch Regina, boss?"

"You'll never be him," I hissed. "You'll never… be him."

I took another drink and pressed the bottle to my forehead. I wish I could have at least gotten to kiss them one last time. One more I love you. One more time to make love to them both. But I guess fate had other plans. I wouldn't even get to meet my child.

"Vadim, I've brought…" Regina sighed. "You go, Adrik. I've got this."

I heard Adrik, the replacement sigh and step out of my room. Regina placed the tray on the table and gently took the bottle from me. I let her without putting up a fight. Over the past few months, she's cared for me like a mother would a son. She, too, was experiencing pain from the loss.

"I've brought you something to eat. It's just a sandwich, but the bread should soak up some of the alcohol."

"Eto bol'no." I whispered. "It hurts so bad."

Regina helped me into bed and squeezed my hand. "I know, but I have faith. I pray every night. For you. To bring them back. For hope that they didn't succumb in the fire."

"I-I… fuck, I loved them and now they're gone. What do I do, Regina? What the fuck do I do?"

"You, Vadim Koslov, are going to sober up and eat your sandwich. Rest and regain your strength. Then, you are going to meet with my son and assemble a team to bring them back home, You are a Koslov and you know what that means?"

"I'm going to get my revenge on everyone."

"And what happens if someone gets in your way?" she asked.

"Kill them. Kill every last one of the motherfuckers."

"Good. Now, get some rest. Adrik will be right outside your door if you need him."

"He could never be Alexei." I muttered.

"Vadim," Regina chastised me. "He's not trying to be. He's just trying to make sure you don't hurt yourself. I mean it, get some sleep after you eat your sandwich."

Regina handed me a sandwich and folded her arms over her chest. I took a bite and gave her a pointed look. "Happy now, mother?"

"Lord help me, just make sure you're not drunk when you meet with my son. I need you to be focused and alert to get Alexei and Jules back. And Vadim?"

"Yes?"

"You've always been like a son to me. You may be the boss, but I won't hesitate to knock you on your ass."

Links:

Join my Facebook group

Like me on Facebook

Instagram

Twitter

Sign up for my newsletter